S0-BJA-389

SLATER'S BOOK

Also by James Wyckoff

LARS

JOHN SLAUGHTER'S WAY

SLATER'S BOOK

JAMES WYCKOFF

DOUBLEDAY & COMPANY, INC.

GARDEN CITY, NEW YORK

1976

All the characters in this book are purely fictional,
and any resemblance to actual persons, living or dead,
is purely coincidental.

ISBN 0-385-08662-8
Library of Congress Catalog Card Number 75-14847

Printed in the United States of America
First Edition

For Angus

SLATER'S BOOK

1

I got a lot of it from Uncle L.T., him being part of things like he was. Then the rest, we some of us put it together over the years from bits and pieces—drinks down at the Silver Dollar, a game of stud at the Pastime, an oldtimer recollecting something he'd heard someplace—until the whole of it hung together like one of those Pieces dolls the Sioux make out of things just lying around.

So it wasn't any one person knew the whole, not even Slater himself. And for sure the records never did come to light that was subpoenaed by the governor, and nobody ever did come to trial, not a one of Hinchy's Invaders or the big stockmen. Still, it did get settled. And I will try to tell how it was.

Best of all, from a certain point of view, was Slater's book, the little copybook he wrote in during that day and night out there at the Circle E when he did what he did and no one in the whole of Wyoming and more than likely a few more in the rest of the country, or the West anyways, will ever forget it.

I guess you could say it got started back in the early

spring, or even that winter of '91–92, though I remember Uncle L.T. saying it must've begun way long before that —back when Slater was growing up with High Eagle and the Shoshones. Him meaning that it wasn't so much what happened as it was the way it happened, that being on account of the way Slater was.

Funny thing, though it's still talked about all these years later, nobody ever really wrote it all down. Only the newspaper accounts at the time, and they never got the real straight of it. People were afraid, I guess, least the stockmen were, and the deputies, Hinchy's Army. And too, sometimes it's good just to let things be. Which maybe I ought to be doing . . .

2

That was the spring the snow stayed late in the land. In the Big Horns of northern Wyoming the thaw came slowly, the Greybull chock full and over its banks in places, with the rushing green-gray water and mud and chunks of ice.

There, in the Northwest, the great mountains hold snow on their peaks all summer long, but in the spring the great snows that do melt on the sides of the mountains and in the valleys run down to the Greybull river and are carried through that long cut of mountain range, down through Meeteetse—sometimes taking out the bridge—and on out to the south country. Then, when the swollen river has fed the land, it settles to its banks and winds through cottonwoods and willows and box elders and the long, beautiful land beneath the high, wide sky.

This day the dawn came red over the tops of the mountains, turning to gold as it washed over the town. During the night a light snow had fallen, not wholly covering the ground or the roofs of buildings. Now the morning light touched the whiteness on the buildings and in the street too, holding pieces of it for a moment before warming it to melt and be gone.

A blaze of sunlight stroked the cold window panes of Henry Sayles' General Store and paused on the silver conchas on the saddle of a steaming dun horse standing with four others outside the Silver Dollar.

A dog barked. And now the morning light touched the unwashed window of the saloon, piercing through to some bottles on the shelf behind the bar. But nobody knew it. Four men stood around the potbellied stove, lost in what the rider of the dun horse had to tell.

"Damn fool Tod had to throw down on him." The speaker was a lean, tall man with a heavy jaw. Even so, he moved this with great speed as he spoke.

"Where is Tod now?" asked a heavyset man with a cast in one eye.

"At Doc's getting patched up."

"The others?"

"Rode out to the Z Bar case I missed you in town. They'll be here directly."

Someone let a whistling rush of air out of his mouth.

"Four of you!" The heavyset man stood suddenly tall and hard in the center of the group.

"Look, Canton, I told you from the start I didn't like the idea." The rider, whose name was "Holy" Holley, reached for his glass of whiskey. "Warning him—all right. But I am against killing him, or any of them at this point. And I have said so all along."

Someone in the group said, "Four of you could have cut him right down."

"Holy" Holley turned quickly on the speaker. "I am not

in that line of business, Carl." His eyes were hard on the man who had spoken.

Carl Mattson looked away and said nothing.

"We are cattlemen, not gun hawks. I went out there to offer him a deal, like we had all agreed. Sure, I knew he wouldn't take it. But we had to make the offer."

"To a goddamn rustler!" It was Clyde Canton speaking. And a murmur of agreement passed through the group.

"Holy" Holley reached for the bottle, poured quickly into his glass, getting some of it onto the bar; and downing it in one smooth motion. "He's a rustler, that's a gut. And so are the others. And I don't want them branding our mavericks any more than the rest of you." He ran his eyes over the group, moving his big jaw on the words. "But I do not want a goddamn war on our hands. Those boys ain't backing down at all. And I for one know that better after what I seen this morning."

"We could have Clay Joyner bring him in for that shooting," Carl Mattson said, "swear he drew first."

"Joyner is one of them, so forget that." "Holy" Holley refilled his glass. "I am telling you, Tod throwed down on him, and by God he got his thumb shot clean off." He shook his head, his deep-socketed eyes reliving the scene. "I never seen anything like it. He could just as easy shot out a eye or a toenail!"

A man wearing a dark brown stetson hat said, "Hell, if he won't negotiate—I mean, he's one of their top men—then what in hell you recommend? We want to know, Holley. Tell us. We can't negotiate, we can't kill them, what you want us to do? Sit around while they pick us dry of our beeves? Hell damnit, it's the law. The bill was passed five years ago—no branding without one of us from the Association being there. It's the law; and they're clear rustling. And I am for hanging or shooting the sonsofbitches, every last damn one of them, and I mean right now!"

Silence followed this outburst. Behind the group, the bartender, a baldheaded man with a blue bandanna around his throat, was slowly wiping the bar, an operation he had been engaged in for the past several minutes as he pretended to be deaf to the conversation. There was nobody else in the saloon at that early hour.

"You don't want a war," the man with the brown hat resumed in a calmer voice, "but it is coming to that. These small outfits, them goddamn rustling bastards are stealing us blind."

"They all act like they think it's still the old days," said another man, a man with iron-gray hair. "They just got no respect for the law, or private property." He spat vigorously into a nearby cuspidor. "Clyde, what we gonna do, go on waiting?"

"No. We will not wait," Clyde Canton said. "But we will have to take it up with the men in Cheyenne."

"But roundup is due and they're dropping calves right now. They'll be out there with their irons and if we ain't along with something . . ." It was the gray-headed man who had just spoken to Clyde Canton. His name was Hard Winter Hayes. He had somehow earned his name during the terrible winter of '86–87 when the whole country had frozen into a sheet of ice and the herds had starved almost to extinction.

Clyde Canton ran his long forefinger slowly across his

long mustache. "We will get them," he said quietly. "We will get him." And he emphasized the last word. "We will get him and it will break the rest of them. We take one of them like that, one of their top men, and the others will have to fold."

"But how?" Carl Mattson asked. He had one of the biggest spreads in that part of the country. "How are we going to get him? I mean, we got to get him good, get him so he is finished." And he looked at "Holy" Holley. "Maybe we have to kill him."

"Holy" Holley had a lot of wrinkles in his face, and they all seemed to let go as he said after a pause, "All right. But it has to be right with the law. I do not just mean Clay Joyner's law."

"How could it not be right?" asked the man with the brown stetson hat. "We are in the right. They are the ones breaking the law. Not us."

"But how?" said Hard Winter Hayes. And he scratched deep into his thick gray hair.

"There is a way," Canton said softly. His eyes were on the window that faced the street.

"Holy" Holley squinted at Canton. "What do you have in mind?"

A trace of a smile touched the cattleman's eyes, but his mouth remained hard. "There is Molly Durham," he said. "You have forgotten about Molly Durham."

It was in the following silence that the bartender spoke. "Rider coming down the street." He was standing at the window, looking out, and spoke over his shoulder.

Two of the group joined him now. A rider on a blue roan horse was coming down the street at a slow walk. No one said a word as he passed the saloon and rode on toward the other end of town.

Turk Peabody, the man in the brown stetson hat, broke the silence. "It is him," he said evenly, and though he spoke softly everyone heard. "It's Slater."

3

He was a man of thirty-some. Hard to tell. And it did not matter. Some said he was part Indian. It was known that he had been raised by the Shoshones.

He looked it. He was dark, with black eyes and smooth black hair, and he wore his black stetson hat uncreased and straight on top of his head. No one knew much about him for sure, only that he ran about two hundred head up on the North Fork and he could shoot a button off your shirt without burning the cloth.

Slater for sure didn't give a damn what anyone thought. He knew who he was. He had himself and like the rest of us he'd been born, and like the rest of us someday he was going to die. The only question was—how.

He rode now straight through the town, straight up the one street, which was not very long, sitting like an arrow, but easy too, in the old stock saddle; looking straight ahead, yet not missing things, aware of the horses outside the Silver Dollar and the lather on the dun, and feeling the eyes that followed him. It had been a time since Meeteetse had seen Slater; he didn't come to town often.

The roan spooked some as they crossed the bridge with the river roaring right up on the crosspieces, but Slater didn't cuss or take a cut at him.

He rode on through the town until he came at last to a cabin on the outskirts. It was, in fact, the last building before the rutted dirt street became trail.

There were only two horses at the hitching rail—a buckskin gelding and a bay mare, but he knew there were other mounts in the barn behind the cabin. The sun was a cold yellow disc in the bright blue sky as he swung off the roan and wrapped the reins just once around the hitching rail.

About a dozen men filled the cabin, and their conversation stopped when Slater walked in. He crossed the room without nodding or saying anything and sat down on a chair with no back.

The room had a low ceiling and was heavy with tobacco smoke and the smell of men, two of whom were stooping because of the crossbeams. Everyone had his hat on and all were facing toward the jumbo stove. For even though spring was in the land and it wasn't really all that cold they were still in their winter ways.

One of the men who had to stoop because of the low ceiling beams now pushed his hat onto the back of his head and spoke. "There is a rumor the Association will run some guns and deputies along with the roundup," he said, and turning to Slater he added, "Why some of us figured we ought to call a meeting." He ran his thick hand across his thick face, his eyes still on Slater. "Guess we figured right, since we just heard about the doings out at the Circle E."

Slater gave a slight nod, reaching for his tobacco and papers. "They offered to cut me in on their beef if I'd come over."

"And kill you if you didn't." A man named Charles Carew said it. He was a big man, set solid, with big hands and a big black mustache. He was not long in the country but he was well thought of by the small cattlemen.

"About the size of it," Slater said.

"Tod Collum don't know how easy he got off," said a man who was standing near the back wall of the cabin.

And then Carew said, direct to Slater, "You should have killed him."

"Charles . . ." It was the man who had first spoken.

But Slater was already speaking. "Mister, when I want you to tell me what to do I will let you know."

A bleak silence now held those words.

And Slater added, after a beat, "You damn fool."

Outside, one of the horses at the hitching rail whinnied, but nobody in the cabin appeared to notice. Slater was still seated, looking straight at Carew, who was standing by the stove. The big man was looking back at him, a puzzled expression on his face, as though he just now realized what he had said. Then he looked away, his hand reaching to his shirt pocket for his smokes.

Someone suddenly sneezed.

Slater continued to stare at Carew, who took the tobacco and papers from his pocket but then changed his mind and put them back. While the silence gathered.

"Didn't mean offense, Slater," Carew said.

"I did." He looked around at the group. "I am making a point," he went on. "They have got the deal, the whole pack, and we got to play it close. We cannot go shooting them up without their being happy for the excuse to exterminate us." He looked at Carew. "If we do not stick together they'll pick us off one by one." He pulled on the string of his tobacco sack to open it. "Just like they tried this morning."

Now Clarence Cohoes, the man who had spoken at the beginning, said, "It sure don't look like they're aiming to leave us alone. They have got us all on their Black List."

Someone said, "I hear they call it the Extermination List and there's seventy on it!"

"Seventy!" A man standing at the edge of the group barked it out. This was Ridey Durham, an oldtimer who had fought the Indians. Ridey was in his eighties, maybe more, some said, but he was still tough as whang leather and not so damn slow either.

Slater was building his smoke, and now he put the string of the tobacco sack in his teeth and drew it shut. "Anyone wants to run his own brand or has friends want to is on the list," he said.

"Pretty soon we'll have to ask permission from the Association to fart," said old Ridey Durham.

"Canton and them want it all," someone observed.

Ridey Durham spat furiously into the bucket by the stove. "Hell, didn't they build their herds slapping iron on unbranded calves, same as us! Goddamnit, a beef without no brand on him belongs to who gets his rope and iron on him first. That always was the law in this here country and far as I am concerned it will always be. Where in hell do them jaspers get off claiming they got the right to watch what we brand! Who in hell they think they are!"

The old man had grown very red in the face and suddenly starting coughing. Someone slapped him on the back and someone else handed him a glass of whiskey.

"Sonsofbitches!" But he subsided with the whiskey.

Slater struck a match on his thumbnail and now, canting his head to keep the flame away from his eyes, he lit the corn-shuck cigarette.

"What about our beeves?" he said, looking at the others. "That's what we got to get settled on."

When nobody said anything he went on. "We better see it clear. We got to make a plan and stick with it."

"He is right for sure," said old Ridey, glowing from the glass of whiskey. "We don't have a plan, we don't stick together, we got all the chancet of a fart in a windstorm."

Clarence Cohoes now took a swift look at the others, as though waiting for something. Then he said abruptly, "Like I said, Slater, we all heard about the way you handled that hunting party this morning."

"I sure didn't invite them over."

Wry laughter broke in the cabin now and they seemed to loosen.

Cohoes said, "'Fore you got here we had a sort of a meeting." He paused, and again his eyes went to some of the other men. "Thing is, we would like you to head us, head the organization."

"Time's come for us to get organized," someone said. It was a man in the back, standing next to Ridey Durham; he was usually a quiet man but now suddenly he felt that he ought to speak and take part in things.

"And for sure if we don't get organized, like you said, they will knock us off one at a time," said a man named

Franklin. He and the quiet man who had just spoken ran a few head down in Sunshine Basin.

"That is for sure," said somebody else.

"Like they been trying all along."

"What about it, Slater?"

He had been leaning forward with his elbows on his knees. Now, almost without moving, he flicked his smoke into the coal bucket.

Clarence Cohoes said, "They sure ain't going to quit just because you shot off Tod's thumb. They will be out for real now. And—thing is, we need somebody like yourself to rawhide it."

A round of agreement now melted into silence as they waited to hear what Slater would say.

He sat there on the chair with no back, studying it. Thinking how strange it was, for he'd almost been expecting it. Some things were like that, he knew. They were really like the snow. You knew it had to come. You couldn't stop it. You couldn't stop it falling. You couldn't stop it drifting, and eventually melting. But why? Why him? What he only wanted was to be left alone. Couldn't they see that? Or maybe that was what they wanted too.

But he saw that it was as though something had already been decided. What was going to happen was going to happen. And not he, nor anyone, could change it. He had learned a long time ago that a man had to pay for what he was.

And still, even as he was thinking how he did not want it, a plan was beginning to form in him.

At length he nodded. "Good enough."

Someone reached over and closed the damper on the stove. Two or three men opened their coats.

Clarence Cohoes took off his hat and wiped his forehead with his sleeve. "What you figure for their next move?" he asked Slater.

He did not answer right away. He took out his tobacco sack and papers and quickly rolled a cigarette. That is to say, he accomplished the task quickly, yet without haste. It was the way he always moved—economically, with no waste. He struck a match on his trouser leg and held it while the sulphur burned off.

"Like I already said, we got to stick together. Nobody act on his own." He looked around at the group. "I mean that. No taking off on your own. I want that understood."

"I go with that," Clarence Cohoes said.

A murmur of agreement went through the others.

"Carew." Slater cut his eyes onto the big man.

Carew nodded but said nothing. His eyes were on the floor.

"Anything happens, I want to know about it," Slater said.

"Agreed," said Clarence Cohoes.

Slater turned to him. "I do not know their next move," he said in answer to Cohoes' earlier question. "But ours—ours has got to surprise them."

"Meaning?"

"We must not wait for them to make a move."

"How will we surprise them?" Ridey Durham asked.

"They are stronger than us. They are more, and they sure do not mind killing. But we can play it tighter than them and we can move quicker because we are smaller."

"But how?" Ridey stepped to the front of the group to lift the stove lid and spit inside.

"We will run our own roundup," Slater said. "And we

will run it a month early." He paused to let it reach them. "We will start branding a whole month ahead of them."

There was a moment of silence in the cabin and then everyone began talking at once.

4

In the midafternoon he rode slowly from the town. He was hungry but he had not wanted to stop to eat. It would have meant talking. And he'd had enough of that.

As he passed the row of frame houses at the edge of town his eyes wandered to the porch where he had last seen her, and he felt something draw inside him.

For an instant he almost turned the roan, but instead kneed him to a canter to put it all out of his mind. Later. Later maybe, when it was all over. And if he was still around.

The first star had appeared above the rimrocks as he rode across the little wooden bridge that met the trail leading up to the Circle E. Now as the roan picked his way up the steep trail he felt the high mountain air cool on his hands and face, and the odor of sage came sharper.

He allowed himself a moment of satisfaction that the bridge was still there. Formerly it had washed out in the spring breakup. But this year he had put more rocks in the triangular pilings and lashed extra rope to the cottonwoods along the river banks.

It was dark and the stars were numerous when at last he rode into the round horse corral and Tip ran barking to meet him. He led the roan into the barn and stripped him and rubbed him down with sacking and put grain in the box for him to feed.

Slater stood in the barn in the dark, listening; a pack rat scurrying along the log wall, the roan chomping on his feed, his own breathing.

Where will it come from, he was wondering. And when? That morning—it had been night really—when he had shot Collum it had been clear. No time for thinking on it then. But now, now the Association would not make a second formal call. Now the call would be a bullet from nowhere.

For a while he stood there in the barn, listening to the roan, keyed to any irregularity in his movement that would indicate the proximity of visitors. And he listened too to the dog. At last, satisfied that all appeared well, he walked carefully to the cabin.

He moved up on the cabin indirectly, taking his time and stopping twice to listen. Inside at last, with the door shut and with his back to the solid log wall, he listened again. Only the barking of a coyote. He struck a wooden match and lit the kerosene lamp. Some of the tension went out of him now as he built a fire and began cooking his supper.

He had built the cabin and the barn and corral just three years before, when he had moved onto this land and set up his own brand. As he ate his hominy and beans and the canned peaches it came back to him; that winter when he had felled the spruce up by the timberline under the rimrocks and limbed them and snaked each one down the hard, snowpacked trail with Pete, the big bay gelding.

Then in the spring he had built the barn and corral and finally the cabin, coping each log carefully so that it fit snug over the one beneath and the join would not catch water. He used only the ax. It was the only tool he had, save for the big hammer and chisel he used to build the rear wall, which was rock, to protect the cabin from any erosion. He put wood chinking on the inside where the logs met, and on the outside he put manure. It was tight, that cabin. The roof, like the roof on the barn, was made of crossed limbs covered with earth. Later, he had put down a wood floor from old lumber traded for with Frank Owens down at Meeteetse.

Everyone had said he was crazy building so high up on the mountain like that. But the moment he had first ridden into the meadow, he had told himself that that was where he would build. And he was sure she would want it too. He had gone so far as to start a root cellar, cutting into the rock side of the mountain directly behind the cabin.

Except she had not come. She had said no. They had better wait. Wait for what, he had asked. She did not really know—but wait. After all, she was still married to Farkas, even though he was gone, had left her more than a year ago. But he had not argued it with her. He had let it go. He was not one to urge or insist.

It was just when he got up to bank the fire that Tip gave a low growl outside the cabin. Instantly Slater stepped away from the light. Then he heard the horse and rider. He stood motionless as the visitor dismounted outside. No one sneaking up on him, no killer would allow that much noise. Even so, he was careful. He heard the man talking to the dog.

Now the thumping step of someone not very careful in his movement. And a voice called.

"Slater—it's me. Hank Weber."

Slater waited a beat, listening beyond the caller, trying to hear the dog.

"I am alone," Weber called out.

"Come in then."

The man who entered was about Slater's size, but he did not move well; he was clumsy. Hair almost entirely hid his face.

"Riding down from Piney I seen your light," Weber said as he moved to the stove, his hands extended toward the heat while he worked his fingers.

"Have you et?" Slater asked.

"Could use some coffee."

Weber sat down with his hat and coat on and began building himself a smoke.

Slater poured two mugs of coffee. He nodded to the stove. "Hominy and beans. If you've a mind for it."

"Obliged."

They sipped the hot coffee in silence.

Presently Weber said, "Been up by Piney looking over Z Bar beef." He struck a match and held a flame to the cigarette he had built and laid aside while he took his coffee. "Looks to be a big roundup."

"Mulligan still with the outfit?" Slater asked, casual.

"Still there. Still poisoning everyone." Weber laughed, his head jerking back onto his shoulders. He leaned forward now, as though he was collecting something he wanted to say.

Slater gave him time. He could see that Weber had come for a reason. After all, he worked for Clyde Canton and the Association. And too, he remembered that Weber had been close friends with Frank Farkas.

"Thing is, Slater, I'm fixin' to pull out. One of the reasons I come by. I want to throw in with you boys."

"How come?" Slater said it real soft.

Weber looked down at his hands, which were curved around his coffee mug. He shrugged.

"Reckon I can't handle Canton. I mean, you know how he is. All that damn piss and vinegar. It gets old. And I don't go for the way those boys, the Association I mean, is trying to push everyone else out of the country. Hell, I'm a working hand same as you . . ." And he looked directly at Slater for the first time since he had come in the door. "Hell, a man's got a right to run cattle same as them. They branded plenty of mavericks to build their herds and no one said nary a word in those days. Big men just believe they own the whole damn country."

Slater studied it.

"Why come to me?"

Weber took a pull at his coffee. "The word is you're heading the small cattlemen."

"Word travels fast," Slater said, wondering why Weber had really come. Had he come to kill him? There were easier ways. Had he come to spy? But spy on what?

Weber said, "I got no cattle. But I am a good hand. Maybe you could find a use for me."

"Maybe," Slater said. "I will turn it over."

The other man nodded. He seemed to hestiate. Then he said, "I seen some of your brand up on Piney, I mean with Z Bar stuff."

"You sure?" He leaned forward onto the table as he said it.

"I seen the brand clear as I'm seeing you."

"How many?"

"Maybe a half-dozen head."

He did not like the way Weber said it. He waited a minute and then he said, "Put your horse in the barn. You can bunk here tonight."

Weber nodded. He rose and started to the door.

Slater stood up. "One thing, Weber . . ."

The other stopped.

"I don't trust you," Slater said. "You cross me and I will kill you."

5

The Z Bar line camp at Piney Creek lay in the hollow of a long draw. A cabin, a round horse corral, and some cattle pens was all it amounted to. The wrangler had just brought in the cavvy of horses for the day's work when Slater and Hank Weber rode in. There were six Z Bar men on the scene, trail-honed men, well armed and not at all friendly toward the visitors.

Slater ignored them as he rode direct to the cattle pens and, sitting easy on his pony, threw his eye over the critters there. He could feel Weber's strong lack of ease at his side. Weber had for sure not wanted to come, but Slater had insisted and so they had ridden out in the pre-dawn.

He knew that of course it was a trap, but he also knew that the only way to beat a trap was to spring it.

Suddenly a voice called out, "What do you want, Slater? What are you doing on Z Bar range?"

The voice was at his back and he did not turn to acknowledge it, but kept his eyes on the cattle milling slowly in the pens. He could hear a horse approaching. As the steps got nearer he turned his horse. And it was big

Clyde Canton riding toward him. Behind him six men were lined up, afoot; well-spaced, not bunched, positioned so that they could cover the visitors.

"I have come for my beeves," Slater said. "As you knew I would." And he looked at Weber, who averted his gaze. Then he let his eyes go quickly to the trees that lined the top of the draw above the camp.

Canton, not missing this swift glance, said, "You are mistaken. We have none of your critters here." But he did not look easy about it.

"I just seen my brand on more than one or two," Slater said, cold as a fresh deck of cards. "And I believe you know what we do with rustlers in this here country." He paused and then said, "You can tell your men to start cutting them out." And his eyes again flicked to the timberline.

"I will tell my men nothing," Canton said, sitting hard in his roping saddle. "Now get off my range."

But Slater had his .44 pointing right at the rancher's belt buckle.

"You can't get away with that," Canton said. "My men will cut you down quicker'n a cat can lick his ass."

"And my men up there will cut yours quicker."

He watched it hit the rancher, who squinted, refraining from turning to look at the line of trees above them. "I don't see anything up there, Slater. You are bluffing."

Slater's smile was frosty. "One way to find out, mister. Now just tell your men to cut out my beeves. I mean, unless you're aiming on sudden retirement from the cattle business."

The big rancher's face reddened. "Slater—someday . . ."

"Someday—what? You will have someone shoot me in the back, is that it?"

"Someday I will get you good." He was a big man and every inch of him was in a rage.

Slater waited a beat. He had his attention on Canton, but he was sharp to every move of Weber's and the six cowboys. "Just tell them to start cutting," he said. "Weber will help them." And he nodded toward the man beside him, who was almost at the point of fidgeting.

"I don't believe you have got men up there, Slater."

"Think I'd be fool enough to ride in here if I didn't?"

He could feel the sun on his shoulders and back as he studied Canton's indecision. Out of the side of his eye he saw one of the cowboys starting to edge toward the protection of a nearby wagon.

"Get back there!" he called.

But the cowboy decided to make a break for it. Swift as a snake, Slater pulled the .44 away from Canton and with one sure shot dropped the man where he was.

Canton had swung off his horse and drawn his gun. Slater, in one flowing motion, brought his .44 down on the rancher's wrist, smashing the weapon to the ground. Now one of the cowboys fired, and Slater, still smooth as silk, made his second score. The remaining men froze. Canton, his face twisted in extreme pain, swore helplessly: his wrist was hanging loose, like an old cloth.

"I hope I broke it," Slater said. "I intended to. You are lucky I didn't kill you." He looked at Weber, whose mouth was hanging open. "Start cutting out them cows."

After a moment Canton had control of himself. "I knew you didn't have men up there, Slater."

"But you were not sure."

"I will be next time. I will kill you next time."

Slater said, "Excepting, it ain't next time, Canton. It is this time, right now." He raised his voice so the cowboys could hear him. "Get my beeves cut out of there, and hurry it up. I don't have all day."

It was still the forenoon when he and Weber brought the half-dozen head onto Circle E range.

Weber said, "Canton will kill you for sure, busting his hand like that, I mean in front of his own men."

"Ain't that what him and you figured for today?" He had pulled rein now and sat his horse facing Weber.

Weber's face had lost all its color. "Slater, I swear . . ."

"Get out of my sight," Slater told him.

"But I never . . ."

"Unbuckle your gun and hand it over."

"Slater . . ."

"I mean right now!"

He sat there on his pony, watching Weber ride out of sight. And when he later rode into the meadow where the cabin stood he knew that he could no longer be alone. He was committed, and there was no going back.

6

Clyde Canton had already scored, however—in another way. Slater had not known it, but Molly Durham had watched him as he rode out of town on the day of the meeting with the small stockmen. Quite by chance, she had been standing at the parlor window of the white frame house when he had suddenly ridden into view.

"Who is it?" a voice behind her asked, and Molly realized that her back, her whole body, had tightened, and she caught her breath at the sight of the rider.

"It's Slater," she said, not turning around.

Behind her, Ridey Durham said, "Headin' here? He was at the meeting."

Molly shook her head. "No. No, he is not coming here."

Now Slater was out of sight and she turned to face the old man who had just entered and seated himself at the table.

"You know tomorrow is your birthday, Grandpa."

The old man snorted. "A whole year younger, by God." And he released a chuckle from deep in his chest.

He stood up now, rather quickly. He was a good-sized

man, bony, and his long bony hands hung down far from the cuffs of his hickory shirt.

"But I do hear horses," he said all at once and cocked his head. "Two, I'd put it."

The girl turned back to the window, brushing a few strands of brown hair from her forehead. Two riders had turned off the main street and were coming toward them. She felt her grandfather standing beside her, and realized how he always smelled of tobacco.

"Clyde Canton and Hard Winter Hayes," he said. "Wonder what them buzzards are after." And he looked sideways at Molly, studying for a moment her soft profile and the set of her long, dark brown hair.

He had always liked the way she stood. Like her mother. For a moment his thoughts touched his daughter whom Molly resembled so. Even after so many years it was hard to remember she was not there.

The old man and the girl watched the two riders dismount. And when the firm, loud knock came, Molly brushed her hair again from her high forehead and went to the door.

"Wanted to have a word with you, Molly," Clyde Canton said in his big voice, entering first and removing his hat.

"Come in."

They entered all the way then, nodding to Ridey Durham.

"Ridey . . ." Canton's look was the one his men took to mean they were excused.

But Ridey Durham was the kind who always ignored such amenities from people like Canton.

"Grandpa . . ." Molly turned to him. "Would you take a look at Tommy?" And then she walked back into the room, offering her visitors chairs with a gesture of her hand.

Old Ridey sniffed. He placed one hand inside a yellow suspender. "The boy is all right," he said. And he made no move to leave.

"We have private business with your granddaughter," Canton said, firm yet with a smile to take some of the sting out of it.

"Please, Grandpa."

The old man snorted, but he could never really go against her, and he didn't want to make it difficult for her either. He turned and left the room, scowling at the two men, who had seated themselves.

Now they relaxed. Canton smiled again, while Hard Winter Hayes looked about, taking it all in. He was a stocky man with heavy, gray hair that came low on his forehead and seemed to make his eyes look even deeper in their sockets than they actually were.

"I will come right to the point," Canton said, leaning slightly forward. And his use of the first person was not lost on Hard Winter Hayes, who scowled. "As you know, I am connected with the school here." He paused, while Molly nodded slightly. "And your son—er, Tommy is it? —will be attending."

"That is so. But not yet. He's still only just a year old." She added the last information with a proud little laugh.

Canton pushed his lips forward and then pulled them back over his large teeth, as though finding difficulty in finding the right way to express what he wished. "Tom

Farkas should be an asset to the school, there is no doubt of that," he said smoothly. "And I am sure that you, as one of the teachers, will be especially proud of him."

"I will be, and I am," Molly said, stiffening. "Only Tommy's name is Durham. Tommy Durham."

"Aah . . ." Canton sat back, sighing, throwing a glance at Hard Winter Hayes and then returning a long gaze to Molly. "It's just this point, Molly, Mrs. Farkas."

"I don't understand," Molly said. But she was starting to, and she could feel something closing inside her.

Canton's voice was even smoother than it had been. "We—well, some of the ladies on the school board feel that since you are Mrs. Farkas, that, well . . ." He let it hang, sitting back in his chair and no longer looking directly at her.

Molly straightened, feeling the shock of it all the way through her body.

"Mister Canton, you know just the same as everybody else knows that Frank Farkas—my husband—does not live here, that he hasn't lived here for some time, and that in fact I don't even know where he is. I do not care what the ladies think. My son's name is Tommy Durham. I want that clearly understood."

Canton was holding up his hand, trying to mollify her. He looked again now at Hard Winter Hayes, his eyes urging the other to speak.

Hayes said, "Yes, we are for sure in sympathy with that. It must be a difficult situation for you. For sure. But Frank . . ." and his voice softened imperceptibly, as though it had been suddenly oiled, yet she caught the change. "Frank Farkas has been gone a good two years now, isn't it?" And he looked innocently at Canton as though for verification.

"I believe so," Canton said, "although Molly—uh, Mrs. Farkas—may correct us." He looked steadily at Molly. "Perhaps," he said softly, "perhaps nothing need be done right now. After all, the boy is only a year old—" And he stopped abruptly, as though he was confused.

Molly was on her feet. "Get out! You get out of my house!"

They rose and the glint of triumph in Canton's eyes showed that he had scored.

"The board, the ladies who actually plan and decide who will teach each year, are of course very concerned about the future of all our children," he said as they went out the door.

She was crying when her grandfather came back into the room.

"What happened? I was out back with the boy. And it sure smells like polecat in here."

"It's time for his feeding," Molly said, and she wiped her eyes.

7

That spring the breakup was heavy. The Greybull was over its banks and there was still more than a hint of the winter that was supposed to be gone. Still, the heavy coats on horses and cattle were shedding and the feed in the meadows and on the mountain slopes was beginning to sweeten. The cows had dropped their calves and soon these would be roped and branded into someone's herd. The question was—whose.

Those men who were immediately concerned with the growth and market of beef were ahorse, checking the herds, studying the feed, the weather, the conditions for spring roundup.

And there were other men concerned, men who did not earn board and found in a cowboy saddle. These men were a long way from forty a month, a war bag, saddle rig, and the clothes a man stood in. These were the big cattle owners, the cattle kings. They too were concerned, especially so this spring.

Since the great Die-up of '87 when the herds had starved and frozen to death these men had lived with a savage memory. Their eyes turned bleak at thought or mention of the frozen beeves piled high against fences, the ganted beasts wandering into towns and eating garbage and the tarpaper from the roofs of houses; and that frightful spring breakup with the rivers way out of their banks, raging torrents of mud and great grinding blocks of ice and countless carcasses of cattle; with the over-all loss in Wyoming alone at fifty per cent.

Sure, the range had been overstocked, but it was the terrible blizzard with the ground covered with iron-hard ice so no steer or bull or cow could paw through for feed that had really brought death to the great beef bonanza.

The weather had beaten them then. But now another threat was pressing. Only this time they would not be beaten. This threat came from the group of small stock owners, cowboys, homesteaders who were building their own herds by branding mavericks.

One day in late March a group of men met at the famous Cheyenne Club. Nowhere else in the cow country was there anything quite as fancy as this gathering place for the cattle barons and English "lords" who came West for sport and dividends and spent the rest of their time in London, New York, Boston, or Philadelphia. The Cheyenne Club boasted the best steward, best chef, best wine cellar of any club in the whole United States. Far from the hot prairie, the icy blast of mountain winter, the saddle sores and necktie parties and cowboy grubline, it was just here in these leather armchairs that the fate of the Wyoming cattle industry was decided.

These men were concerned. Their memories were not short. For sure, the days of the great beef bonanza were long gone. Since then a number of the "lords," the "dudes," had departed, but the hard core of the "Cheyenne Group" was still there and those few men were intending to remain.

At the meeting that day a half-dozen men sat around a table in a private room. Clyde Canton, "Holy" Holley, and Hard Winter Hayes were there from the Big Horn country. With them were Barney O'Toole of the Anglo-American Cattle & Beef Corporation, Horace Tilling of Prairie Export, and Charles Grannel of the Liverpool Cattle Company.

"We thought we should have a meeting," Grannel was saying. "Just the few of us rather than the whole attendance, so we could begin to see our way clear on one or two matters." He sniffed. Grannel was a man of about thirty, a Harvard graduate who had only recently come West when his father, Cyril Grannel, had died, leaving him his legacy. He looked at the "Meeteetse men," as he called them in his mind, and said, "You three must have a lot to tell us." And he glanced at O'Toole and Tilling, receiving their silent agreement.

"We are up there where it is getting into a real tight," "Holy" Holley said. "If that's what you mean. Three men been killed in the past two weeks; I mean, they were caught rustling Z Bar beef," and he nodded toward Clyde Canton, whose brand it was. He was about to make reference to Canton's bandaged arm, but wisely refrained. "But the thing is, the whole county is about ready to boil. You have heard about the roundup."

"We have," Barney O'Toole said. He was a big man, equal in size to Canton, maybe a few years older. He was going bald at the temples but he thought it made him look distinguished. Like Canton, he liked to move fast, to get things done; he had small patience for people like "Holy" Holley who always wanted to "turn it over." At the same time, he was not impulsive at the expense of his business.

Nor was Clyde Canton, who now said, "Then you know they are planning to run their own gather a whole month before the regular, the legal, roundup." He took out a cigar and bit down on the end of it. Looking for somewhere to spit the tip, he finally took it out of his mouth with his fingers and flicked it at the bowl in the center of the table, which was already holding ashes and a cigar butt. Just at this point a white-coated waiter came by and removed the bowl, placing a fresh one and asking if anything was needed.

"More brandy," O'Toole said without looking up.

"But what has been done about it?" Horace Tilling asked in his precise Scottish accent. "What have you done about the roundup? You realize, we all must realize, that to allow it is to invite ruin." He had spoken, leaning forward on his chubby knees, and now he sat back, opening his hands in an offering gesture while his thick white eyebrows rose toward his hairline and his lips tightened in emphasis of what he had just said. "You know," he went on, "my directors, Prairie Export, are very concerned. Something has got to be done." He leaned forward again, suddenly, to receive the glass of brandy that the waiter had brought. He raised it in a swift, wordless toast and drank. After which he belched softly and patted his round stomach affectionately.

Hard Winter Hayes accepted the cigar offered by O'Toole now, but he did not light it. He held it in his hand and pointed as he reviewed the steps taken by the three of them. "As Holley told you, three men were caught rustling and were shot. Then we put some spies out. See," he put the end of the cigar in his mouth and now spoke around it, "we feel the man to get is Slater. He is their leader."

"Then kill him," The words fell on the table like a bullet. After a short pause, O'Toole added, "After all, he is breaking the law."

"We have threatened him, tried to bribe him," Canton explained. "But to kill Slater outright, we might have a war on our hands. Not that there is any great love between Slater and the others, but they rely on him, they need him. They have the sense to know that, and they will back him."

Grannel said suddenly, picking it up, "What do you mean, no great love between Slater and the others?"

A smile broke on Canton's bony face. "The thing is, Slater is quiet, stays with himself, not social. He is a strange man, the sort a man feels uneasy with." He paused. "For sure, not a man to get previous with."

"He is too goddamn independent is what you mean," burst out Hard Winter Hayes. "And that's a gut! He just don't give a damn for anyone!"

"Story is he was raised by the Shoshones," Canton said.

"And some of it has rubbed off?" suggested O'Toole, brushing ashes from his sleeve.

"Holy" Holley snorted. "More than some, I would allow."

"But he has his weak point, just like anyone else," Canton went on.

"A woman, I take it," Horace Tilling said smoothly, and his soft white hand traveled swiftly to his glass of brandy, which he lifted with pleasure. "I am correct, am I not?" And he cocked a laughing eye at Canton.

Canton coughed out a laugh and proceeded to tell the company a racy story. A roar of appreciative laughter greeted the punch line. And after a pause for drink the seriousness of their situation bore in upon them once more.

Clyde Canton said, "Well, it was like that with Slater and this Molly Durham. She lives now with her child and her grandfather, and for some reason or other she has been allowed to teach school. . . ." He let his sentence hang in the air while, with his tongue pushed deep in one cheek, he looked around at the group.

"It is a point, without question," Charles Grannel said briskly. "No question. And you must pursue it. But at the same time . . ." He raised his hands. "We must act quickly. As I see it, and I am certain you are in agreement, the country wants to be rid of the rustlers once and for all. We have been too easygoing. Much too easygoing. Now is the time to step in and really get it settled. For everyone's benefit."

"Holy" Holley, nodding as the waiter offered further brandy, now said, "That is certain. We cannot delay. At the same time, we cannot encourage a county uprising."

"Why not?" It was O'Toole, leaning forward on his knees now, stabbing his thick, almost square-tipped middle finger onto the tabletop where liquid had spilled and stirring it into a little puddle. "Why not stir an 'uprising,' as you call it, or better, an 'insurrection?' As I see it, there already is a state of insurrection up north. And maybe it—uh—needs to be controlled." He sat back, his eyes partially closed, shrewdly taking in the others.

"Holy" Holley said, "I am thinking you have got something up your sleeve."

O'Toole's lips tightened behind his short mustache and he nodded his head several times, short, quick little nods. And then he said, "Gentlemen, nothing ever gets done by a committee. I think, as cattlemen who have achieved a rather large measure of success, you will agree."

"Committee talks it all to death," Hard Winter Hayes said dourly, and he scratched himself.

"Then," said Barney O'Toole, "you will perhaps understand why some of us, a few of us, have already entered upon an arrangement, a plan that will, shall we say, regulate the situation in northern Wyoming and will rid us of every rustler." He reached into an inside pocket of his fine broadcloth coat and drew forth a white piece of paper. "I have here the list of those who must be dealt with. We need to go over this list very thoroughly so that we do not make the mistake of including innocent persons. And," he added, "there may be others we would wish to add."

From another pocket he took out another paper. Laying it on the table before him, he tapped it twice with his forefinger. "And here, we have the details of the plan which will settle the rustler situation." And with his lips pursed and with a lively glint in his eyes he looked around at the group. He had certainly brought their interest to a peak. Which was just what he had intended.

8

It was April now but suddenly the spring that had been promised seemed far from the land. A cold snow fell on the first and the wind was wicked in the mountains.

"It's gonna be a rough roundup—a whole month early," Nick said.

"Rough or smooth, it is going to be," Slater told him.

Nick had moved into the cabin a few days earlier. He was a young man, a boy really, sixteen, and he had helped Slater with the stock from time to time. He was, in fact, Molly Durham's cousin, and Slater was glad to have him there on the ranch.

Now it was that news of the three men shot by Z Bar cowboys came. In the person of Clarence Cohoes. Slater and Nick were wiring poles in the horse corral when he rode in.

"The Association said they were rustling," Cohoes reported.

"What were they doing on Z Bar range?" Slater asked. "Didn't I make it clear that no one should put out on his own?"

"You did. And you ain't any madder about it than I am."

"You tell them, Clarence, if it happens again I am pulling out."

The old man spat decisively at a clump of old horse manure. "I am with you, Slater. And so are the others."

Later, he had watched sourly as the cattleman had tightened the cinch on his dappled gray and then mounted and rode off.

Nick said, "When you figure to start roundup?" Cohoes had come early and they had all breakfasted on dry-salt meat and eggs. Now the two of them were having more coffee.

"We'll start the gather next week," Slater said. "Sooner if we can get ready."

He finished his coffee now and rose. "We'll saddle up then. I want to take a look at the feed over by Willow Creek."

They rode in silence under a cold sky as bright as metal. And they rode easy, allowing their horses to pick their way over the bony trail. But he was alert. He knew that he could not let down for an instant. And at one moment he was sure he saw a horseman up on the rimrocks and he had an idea it was Weber. When they came lower into the valley and the going was difficult because of the mud, he found himself wondering again about Weber.

"Stock looks pretty good," he said to Nick as they pointed their ponies back to the ranch. "'Specially the he-stuff is looking all right." He spat, aiming at a clump of sage. "And the feed's coming up. Just hope it don't snap in sudden cold on us."

The sun was getting close down to the rimrocks by the time they rode into the corral.

"Company," Nick said, spotting the claybank gelding ground-hitched near the barn. He looked sideways at Slater. "Did you know?"

"Seen him from when we was up in the timber," Slater said. And he added, "You better start noticing, boy, I mean if you want to get old in this here country."

The boy's cheeks colored. "Wish you would teach me some things," he said as he got down, grounding his reins.

"Man's got to teach himself."

"But I mean—like they say . . ." and he paused, and then went on, "like they say you used to live with the Shoshones."

Slater stood square in front of the boy, who was now reddening even more. "I will tell you one thing," he said. "And it is this. You make too damn much noise. I mean inside. You got to learn to listen better. Or more sooner than later you'll likely take up permanent residence in the country."

It was old Ridey Durham who now came walking toward them from the outhouse, adjusting his wide, brass-colored galluses. Tall, bony, with his long bony hands hanging far out of his cuffs. He wore a cloth cap on top of his white hair.

"Figured you had to get back sometime or other," he said, chewing rapidly on his plug of tobacco.

Slater nodded. He had known Molly Durham's grandfather for a long time, had worked with him more than a bit.

"Got to talk to you." Ridey looked at Nick, nodding a

greeting to his young relative by marriage, and added, "Alone."

But the boy, sharpened by Slater already, had gotten the message and was already turning toward the horses.

"We will go inside then," Slater said.

In silence the two men walked to the cabin.

Slater heated the coffeepot and they sat at the table.

"Don't know if you know how bad it is in town, Slater," the old man said. "Especially since the last killing."

"Only what I would expect it to be. Everybody liked Jake. He will be sore missed."

"Three now. Everyone is askin' who is next."

"Nobody has to be next," Slater said, hard. "I warned against us working on our own," he went on. "You were there, you were there when we agreed we had to work together or they would pick us off one by one. Those boys should have waited for the roundup."

"That's what I know. Still, it is a tough one. The town is pulled in tighter'n a bull's ass in fly time, I'm telling you."

Slater said nothing and Ridey went on. "It's sure because of us announcing the early roundup too. The Association don't like to take that kind of a thing lying down."

"Didn't expect they would."

Slater poured coffee. He could see that the old man had something else on his mind.

"Coffee's hot." The old man whiffled into the cup to cool it. "They paid a call on Molly," he said then.

"Who?" And he felt himself close on the word.

"Clyde Canton and Hayes."

"What did they want?"

"What they want is your hide, and they do not care how they get it, or who they cut down in the way."

Slater said nothing.

"They are going to cut her out of the school. Not let her teach." Ridey took a noisy swallow of coffee. "Oh, the polecats started off real smooth. Said how the ladies on the board was looking forward to seeing young Tommy Farkas when he got old enough; and how they wanted to sign him up right now, even though he had three more years 'fore it was even time for him to start. Course, Molly corrected them on the name to Tommy Durham, which was what they was after."

Slater had taken out his barlow knife, and now, leaning forward with his elbows on his knees, began whittling a stick.

"Like I say, they pointed out how Frank Farkas had such a fine boy, and asked his *exact* age and mentioned how long it was since Frank had been up and gone. I mean, no chance not to get the drift of it."

The old man looked around for a place to spit, then let fly at the stove bucket. "Then the old ladies began cutting her on the street. You know, those old biddies with their faces all screwed up like they just swallowed a pint of neat's foot oil."

"So it is all over the place."

"And this morning one of them told her they wasn't sure about her working with the school next year. Said they might have to cut down."

"How is she?" he asked.

"Like always."

After a pause Slater said, "She is what most people ain't."

Old Ridey cut his eye swift at Slater. "It will be tough on the boy," he said.

"She know you are here?"

"I told her I was riding up to my old cabin on Spring Creek, which I will be doing now. Want to see how it is, what with those damn Z Bar riders about." He cleared his nose and rubbed it with the palm of his hand. "And I want to see they don't get their lunch hooks into my dynamite sticks."

"I thought you were going to bring me some for my root cellar," Slater said.

"Plumb forgot. But I will do just that."

"You be careful." And Slater heard a harshness in his voice that he had not intended. And he said again, still firm, but more gently, "Take care out there is what I mean."

"Guess they figured on splitting you and the rest of the men," Ridey observed. "Far as I can see, they are all right along with you."

"We will see how they are when things get tight, like they surely will. It is only just started."

They sat with this for a moment or so, each silently turning it over. From out near the barn came the sound of Nick cutting firewood.

Presently Slater got up and lit the kerosene lamp. "You'd best bunk here tonight," he said. "And go on to your place in the morning."

"What you figure they will do next?" Ridey asked by way of accepting the invitation.

"Next?" He had been thinking of her and the boy, and now the old man's words pulled him back. "What they will do is easy enough to figure. You know it same as me. They will really start killing us."

9

The night was cold and clear and he lay in his bedroll on the pine needles across the clearing from the cabin, smelling the pine and fir and spruce, and, whenever the wind stirred, the blue roan who was staked with a picket pin nearby. And he listened to the night sounds in the tall timber around him, and in the earth too, and now and again the roan's movement.

He had decided not to sleep in the cabin for fear of unwanted callers in the night. This way he could hear an approach, and the pony was close if he needed to move in a hurry. He had left Nick in the cabin, for it was not the boy they would be after; and if they did try him, he could cut down on them more easily from the timber.

Now he lay still, listening not with his ears so much as with his body, his whole self. The way High Eagle had taught him. Yes, it was the right way. It was good lying there. All the things were there that a man needed; except people, and he was not sure he needed people. So strong it was, the silence which was not silent. So much stronger than anything he could imagine really that it was like a different sort of sound, like a chord striking through his whole body. And he did not try to do anything with it; he wished only to know this taste of peace, of harmony from which for such a very long time he had been lost.

In that way he lay there through the night, sleeping and waking, almost as though it was one thing; his mind quiet, knowing that harmony in him still, that motion inside that was also a stillness.

Since when had it been gone? Since the time with High Eagle's people. Since that summer when he had first known her. How long ago? Pretty young he had been, when he had first met her down at the New Year's dance.

She was sure pretty. He had asked her to dance, and he knew he had been like a heifer, half drunk from whooping it up down at the Pastime with the boys, and tromping all over her feet. He'd been glad next day that he'd remembered to take off his stetson hat and he'd had a clean shirt on.

Then she was gone, or dancing with someone else, or something, and he was feeling the heat and the drinks and starting to get a little sick. Then, lying in the back of Roy Martin's wagon on the way up to the sawmill, where he'd been helping Roy get out building logs for Charlie Kendall, he had wondered who she was.

And he hadn't seen her since. But he'd thought of her, thinking how awful he'd been at the dance, and wanting to find out who she was, and see her again, but afraid to, afraid maybe that she'd remember him and how he'd been.

Until that spring when he'd been out wrangling horses for the Box 4 and he was over by Spring Creek and she'd come riding up that draw in the late afternoon with the sunlight slanting on her, riding a little strawberry roan with a white blaze on his forehead. And he'd felt all his insides stop and he got real light for a minute.

He had been riding a big hammerhead sorrel, and what with him getting spooked at just about everything and himself with his bum leg from slipping when he was busting a calf on roundup a while back, he was having a fistful. The sorrel had come near throwing him a couple of times.

How clear it all was, all the years after, how the sunlight had been on her hair and her smiling right at him. And he had felt the sun on his shoulders, warm, and on the backs of his hands.

He had thought, after the dance, that maybe she was some dude girl, maybe a daughter of one of the English "lords" who were buying up everything in the cow country. But no, he had seen right off that she knew what she was doing on that pony. She was riding a regular stock saddle and she sat in it like she was planted there.

She was Tom Durham's daughter, a widower who ran the hardware store in town and was one of the big men around. And that was how it all got started.

That summer he had ridden out to see Molly just about every evening. They never met in town. There wasn't anything to do there anyway. They used to meet down by Spring Creek and sometimes Molly brought along some supper. And they'd ride up to the timberline or maybe sit on a knoll and not talk much but just look out over the long, deep valley with the Greybull roaring big below, and the outfits downcountry, and higher up, all around them, the mountains strong in the sky, gray; the far, highest ones white. And the big sorrel and the roan nearby cropping the short buffalo grass and now and again kicking at a fly or biting an itch. All summer long.

And then one evening she didn't come. He waited a long time, until it got dark and he felt the chill of the coming winter in his shoulders and thighs.

Next evening she wasn't there either. He had thought to ride into town to see, but he knew she wouldn't want that. And he would not have gone anyway, being the way he was.

Then the third night he got to the creek early and she was already there. It was a while coming out. Her dad was sending her to school back East. He had found out about her riding out in the evenings.

She had cried and he had held her to him. "I will come back," she had said. And he had told her he would wait. "I will be waiting," he had promised.

And he could hear it now, now lying in his bedroll on the pine needles, staring up through the tall trees to the stars that covered the sky.

A year later Tom Durham had been thrown from a wagon when the team bolted, and broke his neck. And so Molly was alone, except for her one grandparent.

When she came back West, she came with a husband. Frank Farkas was a gambler, land speculator, and, some said, gunman. He did not take long to go through the family inheritance, which was not small. Tom Durham had been wealthy.

It was Ridey explained it to him. "I will tell you the

straight of it, boy. Tom didn't want his daughter hooking up with no Indian, half or full."

Slater had said nothing; for somehow he had already known that. It had not even occurred to him to tell Ridey that he was not Indian, at least not by direct blood. He would never explain himself.

But the old man knew the way it was. "I am only telling you, son."

"And Molly?"

"Molly is young. She always did what her paw wanted, being as she never had no mother." Then, "She ain't happy. I tell you that. But she will stick by what she done."

So long ago. And it was all right here, right now with him. He looked up again at the great sky, just as he had that night they had said goodbye. The sky then had been covered with stars and he remembered how as he rode away alone he had looked up and wondered how long they must have been up there.

Now he slipped into sleep again and when he awakened the sky was lightening for a new day. He was hungry. It was cold. In a little while it began to snow.

He lay there for some moments, reflecting. It had come to him sometimes that he might someday return to the Shoshones. He even wondered why he had left. Blood? Except, what was blood? He was not Indian, and yet he knew he really was. In a certain way. Only, what was he really? Where did he belong? Here in white country? Or there with High Eagle's people? Or was it maybe some other place?

Around the middle of the forenoon the snow stopped and it began to fair off. He was out in the corral soaping his saddle and bridle with neat's foot oil when he heard the rider coming. He stepped into the barn for cover, taking the .44-40 Winchester with him.

It was Clay Joyner, the county sheriff who rode up, and he sure did not look happy.

10

Clay Joyner was a man of fifty, old for the kind of life he had led. He was one of those men who always look the same—old, worried, tough. He had been, as a young man, a pretty nifty road agent. Out around Oro City and Lewiston. His past was known in the county but no one thought much about it. He had, in fact, been "hired" because of his prowess with guns. But he was not the hawk he had been; mostly due to a bullet that had smashed his right hand and for a while had totally paralyzed it. After some months the use of the hand returned, but it had lost forever its suppleness with a sixgun. He was an ordinary gun now, but still long on guts.

Apart from this, he was getting older. However, the chief reason for switching to the side of the law was that his girl had become pregnant. It was a true romance. She was a lot younger than himself and he was crazy about her. They were married in Denver, and when the sheriff of Big Horn County had died, as the saying goes, "from lead poisoning," the citizens, and principally the big cattlemen, had urged Clay Joyner into the sheriff's office. The vote had been a formality, with all that interest behind him. And he had wanted to settle down.

Of course, the big men had assumed that they would have their own man in office. And now they rued the day they fell into that error. For the sheriff was his own man; they learned that fast. Of course, this earned him a place on the Black List.

He swung down from his saddle now and loosened the cinch.

Facing Slater, he said, "Things is ready to boil over in town. We are going to have a war."

"Sure appears like it."

"I want you to help me, Slater."

Slater said, "Are you talking for the Association?"

"I am on the Black List same as you."

"Good luck then."

"They know that I have not throwed in with your outfit." He added, "And I am not going to."

"Who are you throwed in with?"

"The law."

They were out in the corral, squatting on their heels, the way men do when they are outdoors and want to talk things over.

Slater suddenly spat at a clump of fresh horse manure. "Sheriff, the law in this county, in the whole state, for the matter of that, is the law of the big cow outfits. You know that same as me."

Clay Joyner picked up a twig that was lying near him on the ground. "I am not speaking of that law. I am trying to keep the peace in this county. What I was elected to do."

"Good enough. Except how? Sure, there's a war coming. Man can't earn a living in the country anymore, and his life ain't safe. So, how you going to keep it peaceful? It is them you ought to be talking to—not us."

Joyner snapped the twig between his hands and tossed it away. Turning his head to one side, he blew his nose between his thumb and forefinger, sniffed, and then reached for his cigarette papers and tobacco bag. It had suddenly crossed his mind that Kate was baking that afternoon, and for a moment he had the wish to just ride on home and be shut of the whole damn thing. But his horse, the steel-dust gray, suddenly pawed the ground near him and he said, "Mind if I grain him?"

Slater stood up, nodding toward the barn. "Oats and corn in the bin," he said. "The spring is yonder." He started toward the house. "Come in for coffee when you're done."

When Clay Joyner came into the cabin Slater offered him coffee and sourdough biscuits. And they sat there with the morning sun on the windows.

"I have already spoke to 'Holy' Holley," Joyner said.

"Holley's all right. He is a man looking after his interests, same as you and me."

"I don't figure him for killing. I mean, like Canton and Hayes and them others. But he is solid with them even so. He will go along with them."

"Holley didn't build his brand by giving away beeves," Slater said.

The sheriff put down his coffee and finished chewing the biscuit he had in his mouth. "I want to call a meeting between you and Holley and some of the others too."

"You sure got more salt than sense in you is all I kin say."

"I believe Holley would meet."

"And Canton?"

The sheriff shrugged.

"And the Cheyenne bunch? Joyner, you are plumb crazy."

"Slater, my job is to keep the peace. Maybe it ain't the law as a lot of people see it, but that's how I figure it. Maybe I am crazy, but I don't see letting this thing bust all over the county if it can any way be stopped. Hell, there is women and children in the county now. It ain't like it used to be when there was just buffalo, sage, and Injuns."

He stopped and seemed to catch himself, looking sideways at Slater. "I mean, it is different now. Listen, between you and me, I seen this kind of thing before. I was down in Lincoln when the Kid was there and the whole Territory was locking horns over the damn cows. I know what can happen. I seen it!"

"But they will not meet," Slater said. "You know that. They figure they are the law. They believe in what they are doing because they think they are right. They are—" and he paused, "they are *just* men. They are soaking in their justice like a barrel of barley soaking for the pigs to feed on. And they stink the same."

"I know, I know."

"Maybe I will tell you something. I have seen this thing too." He looked down at his hands lying on the table before him. "Justice! Go out and listen to the tribes. They will tell you, if you will listen. But who ever listens to a

Indian! They will tell you about justice and just men and the law!"

A strange smile touched the corners of the sheriff's stern mouth. "Sometimes you talk like a Indian," he said.

"And," said Slater, "sometimes you talk like—a outlaw."

The smile did not reach the sheriff's eyes. He nodded and looked down at his coffee cup.

Now he said, "I am asking you to call off the early roundup, and meet with the Association men."

"No." The word was soft, almost inaudible. Yet Joyner knew it was there.

And Slater went on. "They are not only after us, us small cattlemen and cowboys. They are out to get the homesteaders and the farmers too. They want—everything. And me—I for one will stand in their way. Always." He paused, and added, "Someone has got to."

He had been talking with his eyes on his coffee mug, and now after a moment he looked directly at Clay Joyner. "But I hear you. I know what you are saying. I know it is useless what you ask, but I will meet with them. Only it will have to be soon. Tomorrow, the day after at the latest. Because Thursday we start roundup."

In a little while they walked together to the corral. Slater watched while the sheriff tightened the cinch on the gray.

"He is a good-looking animal," he said. And he reached up and opened the horse's mouth and looked at his teeth. "Got some years on him."

"Got him off John Hogan," Clay Joyner said, suddenly smiling. "Game of stud I reckon he will not soon forget." He let fly a jet of saliva, which splattered a corral pole, and wiped his chin with the back of his hand. "He's a good cutting horse."

The sun was just touching the edge of a light cloud as the sheriff rode out of the corral.

11

Every afternoon the regular train from Denver pulled into the Cheyenne depot with its passengers and mail and freight. There was nothing unusual about this. The train's arrival was noted only by those who were immediately concerned with travel or merchandise or news from the rest of the world. But this particular afternoon the train's arrival sent a current of excitement racing through the town. For attached to the train was a special Pullman car in which the blinds were all drawn.

There were passengers inside the car—twenty-two Texas gunfighters plus Major Miles Hinchy, who had gone to Denver to fetch them and who would be their commander in the field.

As Barney O'Toole had put it, the time had come for action. The plan was simple. O'Toole had outlined it carefully to his companions at the Cheyenne Club. Under the leadership of Hinchy, an expedition would invade the north country and serve warrants on the rustlers. Anyone resisting would of course be shot. Frank Domino, a trusted Association detective, had been sent to Texas to recruit gunmen who would be paid five dollars a day, with a fifty-dollar bounty on each dead rustler. Sweetwater John Hillman had bought horses in Colorado so as not to excite suspicion if anyone in Wyoming started working horses so early in the year. For the plan had been put into operation two months earlier, O'Toole explained, back in January.

"We were looking ahead," Grannel said. "And it is a good thing we did."

Clyde Canton smiled in appreciation. "Just like you said, a committee would be talking on it all summer."

"The railroad is cooperating handsomely," Horace Tilling put in. "And the militia has promised not to interfere. Gentlemen, we are going to wipe those bloody rustlers right off the range and bring law and order to Wyoming."

"Hear—hear!" Charles Grannel held his glass high. "A toast to Hinchy's Expedition."

All drink to that.

The train, when finally ready to pull out, was made up of six cars. The horses had been loaded into three stock cars, three Studebaker wagons were lashed to a flat car, baggage was stored in a fifth car, and the passengers traveled in the Pullman.

Considering the great confusion of loading, it was still early when the conductor signaled that all was ready. Fifty-three men were aboard. Nineteen were cattlemen, there were twenty-two Texas gunfighters, five stock detectives, three teamsters, a doctor, and two newspaper correspondents. And Major Miles Hinchy.

An office had been set up in the baggage car, consisting of planks lying across two crates, and a map of the country nailed to a wall. Even as the locomotive whistle blew the train's departure and the great wheels started and slipped and held, and steam hissed from the engine, the commander-in-chief of the Expedition was outlining strategy and issuing directives to his adjutants.

"It is a twelve-hour run to Thornton," the Major was saying as he pointed a pencil at the map. "But we will not pull into the yard." He paused, drawing his upper lip tight over his teeth. "We will detrain here." He stepped forward and the pencil touched a place on the map that had been circled in red. "At Elk Pass."

The Major turned to face his two adjutants. He was a short man, Miles Hinchy. Quite short. Everyone was taller than he, but he more than made up for it, as everyone said. He was in his fifties. He was trim, in good condition. His black mustache was trim, and he was neatly dressed in highly polished Wellington boots, California trousers, and an army shirt from which the insignia had been removed. A cavalry .45 was strapped to his waist.

When speaking he had the habit of slapping his hand against his thigh, especially when he wished to emphasize a point. It was as though he held a quirt, and indeed he might have carried one during the war when he had served with distinction. That was a while ago. He was retired now, but he had good connections and was well-to-do. He was an old friend of Barney O'Toole. He had very white teeth.

His "adjutants," as he chose to call them, stood listening, attentively too, for the Major was a man who demanded attention above all else.

"What time will we get to Elk Pass, Major?" asked one

of the two men before him. This was Sweetwater John Hillman, range detective. He was a very blond man with thick long hair hanging to his shoulders, and a tremendous mustache. He had the appearance of having just come in from a fierce storm. As a result of a loose saddle cinch, he now limped, having nearly been tromped to death, and this had ended his career as bronc peeler, at which he had excelled. His leg pained him frequently and his disposition showed it, yet it also kept him sharp for the exigencies of his present calling. He had small pity for his fellow men.

"We will detrain at twelve o'clock midnight." The Major paused, slapping his thigh. "Exactly. At Elk Pass we will saddle up and head straight for Meeteetse."

"That's a ride," Frank Domino, the second adjutant, said. Domino was a smooth, lacquered-looking man, handsome, dark, clean-shaven except for a small black goatee, and dressed in a new hickory shirt and expensive Justin boots. He looked, the Major thought, as though he would be very good at cards.

"We shall make camp here," the Major said, returning to the map and drawing a circle with his pencil. "At Pitchfork line camp. Rest, check our gear and ammunition. At sundown we shall enter the town and take over."

"Sundown!"

Major Hinchy coughed out a laugh. "Exactly! No one will be more surprised than they. We shall ring the changes on Custer! You will recall, I am sure, how General Custer struck on the Washita at dawn; well, we shall use the same principle, but with our own—uh—innovation. They will be having supper, putting the children to bed, drinking."

"So long as it don't end up like Custer at the Little Big Horn," said Sweetwater John sourly.

"Custer would have whipped the entire Indian nation if he had been supported!" snapped the Major, coloring and slapping his leg. "Reno and Benteen were looking out for their own skins!"

Sweetwater John Hillman blinked. And then he remembered that someone had told him how the Major worshipped Custer. He scowled, annoyed at himself for making the blunder and furious with Hinchy for having such a foolish evaluation of the feisty general.

"Hell," put in Frank Domino. "Time we get to Meeteetse they will be waiting for us. Our takeoff from Cheyenne was about as secret as a fire in church."

"The telegraph wires were cut before this train pulled into Cheyenne." The Major's words were as hard and cold as the man who delivered them.

They were interrupted at this point when the door of the Pullman swung open and the conductor entered. The train was well under way now and the car was lurching on an uneven roadbed, so that they all had difficulty in keeping their balance.

"I want all possible speed, Mister Norris," Hinchy said to the conductor. "We must be at Elk Pass not one minute after midnight, and preferably well before."

"Engineer's pouring it on, Major." The conductor smiled. He had a very mobile face. Clearly he was nervous and eager to please. Never before had he conducted such a cargo.

"Tell the engineer that I expect him to operate above and beyond the call of duty."

"He is doing his best, sir."

Major Hinchy stared at the man. He came from behind his desk and now stood squarely in front of the conductor, who was almost a head taller. He seemed to rise on his toes as he spoke.

"I am not asking the engineer to do his best, Mister Norris, but to get this train to Elk Pass at twelve o'clock midnight!" He continued to stare up into the conductor's bewildered face. Then, with a curt nod, he turned and started back to his desk.

But a sudden lurch of the train sent him flying across the car and he came close to falling. He regained his balance, glared at the conductor, and, without for an instant losing his incredible dignity, walked stiffly to his chair and sat down.

A smile had started on Sweetwater John's face but he stopped it and ran his hand over his mouth as though thinking of something he wanted to say.

Dismissed, the conductor left the car.

Major Hinchy now turned his attention fully on his two adjutants. "As I was saying, the telegraph wires have been cut at Cheyenne. We shall cut them again when we get north." He paused, drumming his fingers on the desk. "I do not expect any trouble."

"Major, when will we give out the warrants to the men?" asked Sweetwater John.

"Warrants?"

"The warrants that are to be served on the rustlers."

"There are no warrants, Mister Hillman."

Sweetwater John blinked. He looked at Frank Domino, who was looking down at his fingernails, and then he looked back at the Major.

"The men will do their duty," Hinchy said. He leaned back in his chair now, his eyes still on his slowly drumming fingers. Then he looked up. "You know, I am just thinking of Custer's famous remark that he was the best friend the Indians ever had. Meaning, of course, that he was ultimately bringing peace to the tribes. And we, we shall be thanked by history and the people of northern Wyoming for bringing peace to their beleaguered land. Hmm—yes. Yes, I am quite sure of that."

After a moment's silence he leaned forward and picked up a pen from the desk. "Thank you, gentlemen."

12

The train was not far from Cheyenne when the snow started to fly.

"We will earn our five dollars," one of the Texans noted dryly.

They were not uncomfortable in the Pullman, and although slightly crowded there was still room for several of the party to stretch out. The majority, however, were addressing themselves to cards and idle conversation.

The two newspapermen were striking it well. Morley, star reporter on the Chicago *Herald,* was an aggressive, nervy young man not yet in his thirties who had picked up a rumor in the stockyards about a shipment of Texas gunmen coming north to Denver. It was no problem to get a go-ahead from his editor. Morley was the sort who in the absence of a story would create one. He had been chagrined to discover another newspaperman along, but when he learned that his very young colleague, Matthew Bellows of the Cheyenne *Leader,* was on his first assignment his mood improved. It would be easy enough to scoop the greenhorn, who was just out of school and who, clearly, would be reporting only the cattlemen's side of the situation. In fact, Morley had only been granted permission to accompany the Expedition because he had promised to do the same.

By now the two of them had made acquaintance with the Expedition doctor, a man of some sixty years, with a penchant for strong liquor, cards, and a sardonic view of life. Elijah Slocum sometimes wondered why he had lived as long as he had, which was not so long; but his years had been difficult ones, and not very happy. Still, he had a great feel for life, and he looked forward to the expedition north. It would certainly be a relief from the humdrum of Cheyenne medical practice.

"Gentlemen," Morley was saying, "we must realize our unique position. We are to be witnesses to history, a moment in history." And he lifted Doctor Slocum's bottle, which he had received graciously, in toast. And drank. "Aah! Good. Very good!" And he passed the bottle to young Bellows.

"It looks more like winter coming than spring," Bellows observed as he took his eyes glumly from the snow driving on the window of the Pullman car. But the drink made him feel better.

The doctor nodded, reaching to retrieve the bottle. He had wide cheekbones and a large nose. "To be sure, it will be just as cold for the rustlers as for us." And then, after drinking, "Maybe more so."

He chuckled. "The question is, can we all stay reasonably well and healthy. That is the question, to quote the bard. Suppose . . ." And he settled himself back in his seat. "Just suppose the Expedition is suddenly hit with an epidemic. Say, something like the croup. Eh?"

He opened his eyes wide and blinked at the two men seated in front of him. "Or what if we were fed sour beans for dinner? Hah!" His mouth formed a great O as he waited for their reaction. "We would be up the creek for fair!" And laughter bubbled in his throat. "You realize," he continued, his face serious now, "how different the course of history would have been but for the presence of certain maladies. Napoleon's army crippled with diarrhea before the gates of Moscow. The British under Amherst attacked by 'flu. A general, a commander in the field suffering from toothache, let us imagine. A throbbing agony! Or a Nelson, fresh from the satisfactions of the previous night with his lady! On such inconsequences does history really turn, gentlemen."

"An interesting approach," Morley said.

"Much more than interesting, my young friend. The brute fact is, and overlooked by all you scriveners, if I may put it without offering unintended offense, is simply this: More battles, more wars have been decided on these conditions by far than ever have been decided by gun or sword or campaign strategy most carefully planned, or even money. Think of it—the most powerful armed force in the entire world—laid low by a simple little bug invisible to the naked eye. Think of that!" He coughed suddenly into the palm of his hand, and reaching to his pocket drew out a red bandanna kerchief with which he wiped first his hands and then his mouth with dabbing strokes. He sighed. "We men are such goddamn horses' asses." He said this softly, like a reluctant prayer.

"I never thought of it like that," said young Bellows.

"I have," Slocum said. "Often."

"But you will see to it that we keep well," Morley said with an engaging smile on his shiny face.

"From everything except lead poisoning," replied the doctor. "Death, to quote the bard once more, is a disease beyond my practice, sir."

Suddenly he reached behind him and with the speed of a gunswift on the draw whipped out a brand-new deck of playing cards. Offering it in his palm, his eyebrows raised so that a mass of wrinkles appeared on his forehead, he said, "Shall we?"

It did not take Morley and Bellows long to discover that Doctor Slocum was talented in a field other than the medical or historical.

By now everyone was discussing the grim prospect of the long, wintry ride from Elk Pass to Meeteetse.

"We will not get there this day at all," said one of the Texans.

"When we do we'll be too played out even for the girls," said a teamster.

"Whole country'll know we are coming, for sure by God."

"They'll be waiting for us with a hot lead supper, more than likely."

"Hell, the wires been cut. And Domino says we will cut 'em again. They won't know what hit them."

"They are all on our side anyways. Most of 'em, that is. They will be joining us. They want to get rid of the damn rustlers too."

Back and forth, punctuated by the riffle of cards, the clink of coin.

Morley, rising to stretch, said, "We will all talk ourselves into a state of exhaustion before we even get there." And he was piqued when Slocum did not react. Morley had spoken just in that manner which he had reasoned would please the wry doctor. But Doctor Slocum was studying young Matthew Bellows.

Morley frowned and began strolling down the aisle of the Pullman car, glancing at the various games as he passed, exchanging a word here and there.

Slocum had been watching Bellows for several minutes. "What is it?" he asked. "A bellyache?" He wondered, as a matter of fact, whether the young man was getting cold feet over the prospect of what lay ahead.

"No." Matthew Bellows shook his head. "No, I am thinking about the long ride—I mean, on horseback."

"You do not ride very much?"

"I have piles," Matthew said.

"Let us hope you are the only one," Slocum said, and he started to look about for his doctor's bag.

In the next car the Major was writing a letter to his wife. He was letting her know how good it felt to be "back in harness." Of course, he did not offer any information on where he was or what he was doing, but he did permit himself to put it that he would be home soon and that "I can foresee no difficulties within the immediate future."

But it was as if fate had decided to call the Major on this intrepid declaration, for at that moment the door of the railway car opened and Frank Domino and another man entered.

"Have a word with you, Major?"

Suppressing his irritation at the interruption, yet swiftly returning, as it were, to duty, the Major put down his pen and nodded.

"What is it?"

Domino said, "This man wants a word, Major. He has something mighty interesting to tell you."

The man stepped forward. He was respectful. Soft at the jowels though he was not old. And his eyes were, for the Major, too close together; they were couched above rather flaccid cheeks. He did not like what he saw. Yet, the man was otherwise presentable. He remembered him now. One of the Texans he had brought from Denver with Domino. What was his name? Farnum?

"Name is Farkas, Major. Frank Farkas." He had a voice that matched his face. It was smooth, careful.

"What can we do for you, Farkas?" For some strange reason, Miles Hinchy was reminded of a man he had bought some watered liquor from years ago in Dodge City.

Farkas looked quickly at Frank Domino as though he was uncertain, but then this passed and he said evenly, "I used to live in Meeteetse."

A spark touched Hinchy's eyes. "You are from that part of the country?"

"Born in Mobile, Alabama. But I lived a long time in Meeteetse. My wife is there. Why I was eager to sign up with Frank for the Expedition. I believe I can be of service to you, sir."

Farkas was evidently more at ease now. And it was true. Frank Farkas was the sort who found his security in talking. His eyes now caught the map on the wall near the Major's desk.

"Let me show you something, Major," he said. And before Hinchy could respond, he had crossed to the map and had put his finger on the area that had been circled in red.

"This here is Elk Pass. We get off here, right?"

"That is correct."

"Shortest route to Meeteetse is by Horsehead Crossing."

"We have already covered this, Farkas. What is your point?"

Farkas suddenly grinned. The Major was surprised to see he had a tooth missing in the middle of his mouth. "The point, sir, is—here." He tapped the map with his little finger on which was a gold ring. "Here is the Circle E ranch. Here is the ringleader of the rustlers. He is holed up here with fifteen, maybe twenty, of his top men."

At this Hinchy rose briskly to his feet and came around the desk. He peered at the map. "What point is that?"

"It is the North Fork," Frank Domino said from behind them. "Slater's spread. The rustlers' headquarters." And he waited, rubbing the palms of his hands together in front of him.

Hinchy stood there, patting his thigh slowly. He turned to face the two men. "You are suggesting that rather than ride directly to Meeteetse we detour by the Circle E ranch."

"That's it, Major." Frank Farkas sniffed. "That is it."

"But that is out of our way. It is a good distance out of our way."

"Only twelve miles," Domino said. "From Elk Pass. We could make it by sunup this morning."

"And surprise the main gang," Farkas said with a soft smile.

Major Hinchy ran his hand along his thigh, then across the back of his neck. "It is a rough trail I'll wager in those mountains."

"It will be rougher, sir, if we move on Meeteetse and Slater and the rest of 'em come at us from the rear. We'll be in a box."

Hinchy had returned to his desk and now he sat down. He said nothing, apparently lost in thought, with his eyes on the unfinished letter to his wife; but he did not see it.

Suddenly he jerked up his head and his hard eyes bore into Farkas. "How do you know, Farkas, that Slater and twenty men are at the ranch?"

The sudden power of the Major's question almost caused Farkas to take a step backward, even though he had been waiting for it.

"Because," he said, "Hank Weber sent me word. Here." And he dropped a slip of paper onto the desk.

Major Hinchy ignored the paper. His eyes were on Farkas, searching the man for sincerity.

"That is right," Domino cut in. "Weber works for us, for the Association. Matter of fact, it was myself sent him to spy on Slater. They think he is one of them. But he is our man."

Hinchy said, "It is twelve miles over rough ground, and the weather is not with us. It will take up time. The town could be warned by then."

"Not if we move fast," Farkas said. "Even if word does get ahead of us, and you said we would cut the lines, we would wipe out the core of the rustlers. With their leaders gone, and especially Slater, the town would fold."

"We will have them cold-decked," Frank Domino said.

After a pause Hinchy said, "How is the approach? Is he forted up there? What is the terrain?"

"That is the beauty of it," Farkas said, reaching for his ace. "There is only one way up, one trail. And they will have every man watching it."

"That is exactly what I mean."

"Except Weber found a way in over the rimrocks. They won't even be looking that way. We will have no trouble at all surprising Slater and his gang."

"And," added Frank Domino, "Meeteetse without Slater will be an apple for the picking. And when Meeteetse goes we have got the whole county."

Major Hinchy opened a box on his desk and took out a cigar. He did not offer the box, but waited, obviously thinking. Then he bit off the end of the cigar and lighted it.

"I see." He pushed back his chair and stood up. "We can make it by daybreak. Very well then." He turned to Domino. "Mister Domino, go and tell the engineer to get some speed out of this piece of iron!"

And he sat down to finish the letter to his wife.

When the door had closed behind them the two men stood for a moment between the swaying cars, while the track flowed beneath them.

"I been waiting a good while for this, Domino."

"That's what I know." The stock detective spat onto the roadbed racing below.

"I am going to kill that Slater!" Farkas raised his head. The snow had stopped and overhead the moon had risen to light the broken sky. "I sure am going to kill him!"

"You do that," Frank Domino said quietly. "And it will be a hundred dollars instead of fifty."

13

It was afternoon when Slater pulled the shoes on the roan and the bay. They came off easy. Then he cut the toenails and filed so there would be no cracks or splits. He put linseed oil on each hoof.

"Let me do one," Nick said.

"You watch."

When he was finished he squatted down in the corral and built a smoke. "It is fixin' to storm some," he said.

"Will we be ready on time?" The boy was sitting on a cake of hard salt that had been well licked by the horses.

"Figure to." As he looked at the sky, sizing the weather, he wondered if he would be hearing from Clay Joyner. Then, with his cigarette in the corner of his mouth, he walked into the barn and put half a can of oats into the feed box.

He stood watching the roan eat, chomping the clean yellow oats with his big teeth. Some of the oats, soaked in saliva, fell from his mouth onto the edge of the feed box.

Slater stood smoking, remembering now when the roan had been foaled. He remembered the day he and Ridey

Durham had run him into the corral and thrown a rope on him for the first time, and a brand, and gelded him. That was the spring he broke him. He'd had a hell of a time sacking and halter breaking him. That pony was real wild. He'd broke well to the saddle though, and later to a rope. He was a damn good cowpony, he'd stand solid when you threw a rope on anything, calf or steer, not giving any slack, and he knew how to cut a beef out of a herd. Slater ran his hand over the brand on the roan's shoulder.

"Want me to hold him?" Nick asked.

"You just watch."

He put a rope halter on the roan and led him out of the barn and tied him to a corral pole. Then he built a fire and fetched his shoeing box and leather apron, and the anvil.

He trimmed the roan's left forefoot again, and filed it flat so the shoe would not wobble. The smell of the hoof shavings was tart in the cold air. Then he heated the new shoe in the fire until it was almost white-hot. He lifted it out with tongs and put it in a bucket of water.

The roan rolled his eyes at the steam and hissing and pulled back on his halter. Slater gentled him and then fitted the shoe, making it the right size with the tongs and hammering it into shape on the anvil; then he burned its outline into the horse's hoof.

He put nails in his mouth so he could reach them easily, and began to hammer the shoe on, hooking the nails quickly over after he had driven them through the edge of the hoof. He clipped the hooked ends off the nails and then filed the points, and buffed the hoof with the rasp so that it fitted tight with the shoe.

While the boy watched he held the foot between his legs, facing the horse's rump and now and again leaning against his side as he worked. The rear legs he laid in his lap. The roan stood well, though a couple of times Slater had to stop to gentle him.

When he was done he built another smoke and said to Nick, "You can do the bay. I got to take a look at the bridge, see if she's still holding." He paused, his eyes straight on the boy. "You take your time."

"I will."

"Be back directly," he said, and he swung the blanket onto the roan. The pony was feeling good and he swelled his belly when Slater cinched the saddle. But he waited and then cinched up tight. A saddle spill was not what he wanted this day.

The bridge was holding even though the river was higher than the day before. He was back at the ranch in an hour. It was almost twilight now and the air was cold and he could feel the coming snow in it. Nick had the bay's forefeet done and was just finishing the left hind foot.

Slater nodded. "Get you a job as a blacksmith when you're too old for poking cows."

The boy kept working as he said, "It's getting dark. I better hurry."

"Leave it till morning," Slater said. "And don't never hurry around a horse. He can stay the night in the barn."

He was about halfway to the cabin when he heard

Nick's cry, and the bay's high whinny. When he got to the corral the boy was on the ground and the bay was kicking out with both rear feet. Something had frightened him and he had stepped down hard on Nick's foot. The boy's face was white with pain.

It took him a few minutes to gentle the animal and get him into the barn. Then he helped Nick up to the house.

"I am all right," Nick kept saying, even though tears of pain were standing in his eyes, and he had bitten his lip so hard he had drawn blood.

Slater cut the boot away and soaked the foot. "Maybe it ain't broke," he said. "I will put a poultice on it to put the swelling down."

He worked quickly, gently, making the boy comfortable on the bunk and wrapping the foot.

"I'll be all right come morning," Nick promised.

"I don't believe it is broke, but it ain't good. It will hurt some tonight." It meant that he would spend the night in the cabin.

"I will be all right."

Slater poured some whiskey and handed it to him. "You earned some painkiller."

After the drink, the boy felt better. "Ridey told me the time you busted your hand and stacked hay with the pitchfork handle in your armpit."

"My armpit is still sore."

"But you got the stack built."

Slater's eyes went to the window. "It is going to storm some."

Nick took another drink. "You learned medicine from the Shoshones, did you?" He asked suddenly, and he looked a little surprised at his own boldness.

Slater was rolling a smoke, smoothing the paper in his calloused fingers. "I knowed a old trapper once had one arm and he built the best smoke you ever seen. Rolled it right on his knee with one hand, by golly."

He struck the match on his thumbnail and lit the cigarette. Then, his head canted to one side with the smoke rising past his squinting eyes, he said, "Boy, you got more questions than a dude."

Nick's face flushed. "I got to make it for roundup."

"You will. If I have to tie you in the saddle."

As he went out, closing the door, the boy felt his legs, which had been almost locked, loosen. He lay there on the bunk, aware of the bedding under him, feeling the warmth of the stove on his face.

Outside, the sky was thick with snow. It came slicing down, long and thin and wet. The dog was sniffing his feet. Now, as he approached the barn, the roan gave a soft nicker and walked toward him. Should he picket him? He decided no, and led him into the barn, where he put hay in the bin. Then he checked his saddle and bridle.

It was dark in the barn but he could see and now he heard Tip move beside him and felt him push his nose against his leg. One of the horses lifted his head quickly, his ears straight up. A pack rat, was it? But he bent to the hay again. Slater reached down and touched the dog.

In the driving snow he and the dog walked to the spring, then circled through the timber back to the cabin. The meadow, so lush in summer, was covered in white.

Now he did catch something. In the timber just above the corral. It sure wasn't Clay Joyner come with news of a meeting; not coming in like that. Silently, Slater slipped into the timber. The snow was coming down in long wet slices.

He was close to the corral now and he could smell a horse. Then he saw the man. He was afoot, leading the horse, circling along a thin trail that passed over the cabin. He stopped now, whoever he was, to listen.

Slater reached down and found a heavy stick. Now he straightened up, drew his .44, and held it in his left hand. He waited. The man ahead of him started to move. He was sure no Indian, Slater decided, with all that noise. He held the stick in his right hand and now he tossed it at the horse.

It landed on his rump and the horse spooked, giving a short whinny. The man started, and whirled, but too late. Slater had his gun jammed into his back, and his other arm around the man's throat. Then he brought the barrel of the .44 down on the man's head.

He let the horse go, carrying the intruder back to the cabin, after first checking that he was alone. It wasn't until he had the man inside, stretched out on his back, still unconscious, that he realized who it was.

"Wow!" said Nick. "If it ain't Hank Weber!"

14

"We are on time, Major!" The conductor was a man who had spent the greater part of his life in self-justification. A nondescript man, a man who would pass unnoticed in even the smallest crowd, he took pains to keep from seeing himself as he was, a person of absolutely no consequence whatever. And now, having first shrunk from the position to which the company had called him, he had finally come around to seeing that this was an important event, that he was a key figure. Maybe—maybe the newspapermen would put his name in their story.

Standing before the desk in the swaying Pullman, he pulled out his watch. "It is just twelve o'clock, and we are coming into Elk Pass."

"It is exactly twelve o'clock midnight, Mister Norris," said Major Hinchy, looking at his own watch. "And since your train is only just beginning to slow down, we must assume that we shall pull into Elk Pass at least five minutes late!"

Dismay covered the conductor's face. "I hope you have had a comfortable trip, Major Hinchy."

"Be good enough to send Mister Domino and Mister Hillman to me." He looked up then as the door opened. "Ah—you are here. Come in. Come in!"

And Conductor Norris was dismissed.

The three men stood listening to the sound of rain on the windows.

"It will be a wet ride," Sweetwater John Hillman observed.

The train suddenly jolted to a stop and the rain sounded louder to the men in the Pullman car.

"I want everyone saddled up and ready to pull out in twenty minutes," said Major Hinchy. "You have told the men that we are riding to the Circle E?"

"Some don't like the idea too much," Frank Domino said.

"Who does not like it?"

"A couple of the teamsters. Couple of the ranchers."

"And the Texans?"

"No trouble."

"The teamsters will bring up the rear with the wagons. Probably getting cold feet at the prospect of hot lead." The Major snorted. "All right then. That will be all. But I want to move ahead with all possible speed!"

Now the rain was coming down in heavy drops.

"Looks like it be going to hail," one of the reluctant teamsters said, harnessing his team.

It took almost an hour before they were ready to pull out. Two of the Texans' horses bolted, and another man was thrown when his horse slipped in the thick gumbo mud. A hame strap broke on a harness.

"I want that telegraph line cut!" Hinchy snapped, riding up and down the train on his prancing horse.

A Texan rode out, cut the wire, and wrapped the end of it around his saddle horn, then dragged it far out into the sage.

"That'll handle it for a good while," he said. And the men cheered him.

Hinchy was furious at all the delays. And he was boiling when Slocum informed him that the Texan who had been thrown by his slipping horse had a wrenched shoulder and sore ankle and would have to ride in one of the wagons.

"Very well! They will have to make room for him among the supplies."

"And so will Bellows."

"Bellows?"

"The man from the *Leader*."

"One of the reporters? Why? Too much booze, eh?"

"He has piles, Major."

"Piles! My God, man, everybody gets piles. How soft they make them these days! Tell him to ride. He must sit a saddle like a man!"

"Major, that boy is in agony. He cannot sit a saddle. It will be all he can do to make it in one of the wagons."

"Send him on to Thornton with the train then."

"He insists on coming. And, Major, don't forget, he will tell the Association's side of things. I am not so sure about Morley."

"Damnit! Damnit to hell! I do not know how I came to be cursed with such an incompetent command, Doctor

Slocum. Damnit! By Harry, a couple of dozen troops of the old Forty-ninth and I would wipe the Territory of every damn rustler and his brother!"

Kneeing his horse, the Major rode to where the men were milling around with their mounts. He looked at the driving sky, the thick mud.

"Mount up!" he barked. "Mount up! A column of twos. Anyone not ready can stay behind. Mister Domino. Mister Hillman. We are moving out!"

Now, like a long, wet snake, the Expedition came together and started out into the illimitable sage. The rain had started to thicken into snow. Behind them, the train engine gave a toot and with much hissing and billowing steam started toward Thornton.

Conductor Norris, like the engineer and foreman, had been sworn to secrecy. But as he stood watching the disappearing horsemen he was thinking of what he was going to tell the gang at the depot and at Doolin's when he pulled in for some much needed refreshment.

15

In the hour before dawn the snow turned into a penetrating drizzle. It got colder. The Expedition shivered and swore and some of the men even wanted to turn back, only there was no place to turn back to. They were all afoot, leading their horses, and some of them had to be pressed into pulling and pushing the wagons.

Matthew Bellows was in agony and the Texan with the wrenched shoulder was suffering too. But Morley took pity on them and offered a bottle he'd had the foresight to bring along.

"Be a funny if this fellow Slater wasn't even there," he said as they were struggling up a particularly steep part of the trail that was ankle deep in gumbo.

"They could sure bury me laughing," the Texan said sourly.

Bellows, slightly relieved because of the whiskey, was trying bravely to keep his end up. "I can see the headlines! Texas cowboy and two star reporters die laughing in Wyoming gumbo!"

This drew only a desultory laugh from the others,

which, since Bellows was a very shy young man, did not make him feel any better.

"Never have I seen it this bad, man or boy." Doctor Slocum had fallen back to the wagon, puffing hard and holding his side. "Hell, boy, we are all going to have galloping piles and pneumonia before we're done with this little holiday."

At the head of the column, "riding point" as the Major put it, Frank Domino and Farkas struggled up the slithering trail.

"How will it be at Slater's?" Domino asked.

"Not so bad," Farkas said. "It is high up and there is a lot of run-off."

"You are sure he is there?"

"Weber said so. You saw his note telling how to come in over the rimrocks."

About the only dry articles were the guns and ammunition. But they were all angry. Hinchy had forbidden a halt and there were to be no fires.

"Helluva lot easier climbing into a widow's drawers than climbing this here," said one of the Texans.

At last they reached the rimrocks above the cabin and now to everyone's relief they began to descend. Farkas was leading, with Domino and the Major directly behind him. Sweetwater John was bringing up the rear of the soggy column.

The sky was just beginning to lighten as they worked their way into the pine and spruce that edged the meadow on two sides of the cabin. Behind the cabin was the rock mountainside and on the fourth side was the barn and corral, and the regular approach to the ranch.

Hinchy immediately sent men to cover this entry.

"There may be guards out," he warned. "So be careful."

Now the cabin was surrounded on its three exposed sides. And dawn was coming. The rain had stopped. The men were exhausted, but exhilarated at the immediate prospect of action. Even Bellows felt better, although he was half drunk from Morley's bottle. Morley, of course, had not plied him with overdoses of good whiskey out of kindness; he was determined to get an exclusive story.

Suddenly a wild thought pressed in on the Major and he cursed himself for having overlooked it. "What about dogs?" he asked, moving close to Farkas so they could speak softly. "Is there a dog?"

Farkas repressed a smile at Hinchy's obvious discomfort at the oversight. "A dog ain't gonna save them," he said.

But Sweetwater John Hillman said, "We have taken care of the dog, Major."

"I do not see horses," Hinchy said. "Or any smoke coming out of that chimney."

"We will know pretty directly," Farkas promised.

"You are sure Slater is here?"

"I am sure."

"And the rest? Where are their horses? Hillman says there are only two horses in the barn. And none in the corral."

"Probably got them picketed," Farkas said smoothly.

Frank Domino moved in on the conversation then. "Are you ready, Major?"

"Tell the men to wait," Hinchy told him. "Send someone to see if their horses are picketed, and how many."

They waited while the dawn stretched across the sky and the meadow lightened. In a short while Sweetwater John Hillman joined them.

"There are no horses picketed, Major. There are only the two in the barn."

"Then," said Major Hinchy, "we must suppose that there are not fifteen to twenty men in that cabin but two at most, and possibly only one."

He let his breath out slowly from between clenched teeth. His face was as hard as the rimrock they had just struggled across as he turned to Frank Domino. "Did you know that there were only two men, Mister Domino?"

"No, Major. I did not. But we have got Slater for sure. They tell me that is his blue roan in the barn."

"Mister Domino, you will place this man under arrest. Take him back to the wagons and put him under guard." Hinchy had his cavalry .45 pointing at Farkas's belt. "Tie him to a wagon wheel."

"But, Major, it was a mistake," Farkas pleaded. "I thought they were all here. Maybe they were and took off. And, anyhow, Slater is there. He is the man you want. The ringleader!"

Hinchy's voice matched his face. "Fifty-three men, extra saddle horses, wagons, an entire expedition tramping miles out of its way over mountainous terrain just for one man!" His voice rose in spite of his effort to keep it down. "I suspected it. I suspected you had something personal against Slater. Damn you! Damn your eyes!"

He was so angry he was hitting his thigh and almost prancing. "Farkas, I will attend to you when this is all over. You are fortunate I do not have you shot. I shall probably have you whipped on a wheel. Yes. As Custer would have done. And did! My God!" He wheeled on Domino. "Get this loathsome wretch out of my sight. And if he makes any move to escape, shoot him. Shoot him down like a dog!" He was still slapping his thigh furiously as he spoke.

"Major, we still got to get Slater," Sweetwater John pointed out.

Hinchy realized the sense of it, but he was wild at having been duped by Farkas.

"We can get him easy," Frank Domino said.

"Slater has got to be there," said Sweetwater John. "That was his roan for sure in the barn."

"I am told that man can shoot the mouth out of a striking snake," Doctor Slocum said, coming up.

"He will have to shoot faster and fancier than that to get out of this tight," Frank Domino said. And for the first time since they had left the train he felt warm.

16

Inside the cabin, Slater sat drinking coffee. Nick was still asleep. He had awakened two or three times during the night, muttering with pain, but now he was sleeping.

Weber lay in a corner, awake but silent. Slater had questioned him the night before, but all that Weber would admit was that he had ridden out to try once again to work with Slater, and that Clay Joyner had given him the message that there would be "no meeting."

He had tied Weber's hands and feet so that he could get some sleep himself. But now, as he sat with his coffee, he felt a great uneasiness, for he knew there was more to Weber's strange arrival than appeared.

"Weber here?" Nick had awakened.

"I am here," Weber said. "And I would sure like to be untied."

Nick was sitting up. "Foot don't hurt too much," he said. "Maybe I'll make it to the outhouse."

"Use that singletree I brought in for you," Slater told him.

"I'll be walking around like them mountain sheep with

one leg shorter than the other," Nick said wryly as he stood up and tested his foot. "Wonder what they do when they want to turn around and go the other way." He paused at the door. "Didn't tell you I seen one yesterday. A big buck on the rimrock back of the cabin."

And suddenly Slater was on his feet. Where was Tip? He usually slept right outside the door and would be moving about by now. And now at once he knew that something was wrong.

"Don't go out there!"

He had stepped swiftly to one of the windows and was peering outside. Nothing. But he knew there was something.

He spoke too late. Even as he said the words to Nick the boy had opened the door and, leaning on the singletree, had hobbled outside.

Rifle fire crashed from the timber and the boy fell to his knees on the threshold.

Now Slater was at the door, firing with his Colt, and with his other hand dragging Nick back into the cabin and slamming the door.

"I am hit," the boy gasped as Slater helped him to the bunk.

"Don't talk."

"Shoulda listened. I heard you say it, but I didn't listen. . . ."

He had been hit in the chest and legs. While bullets slammed into the log walls and poured through the smashed windows, Slater tried to stop the bleeding.

"You will have to make a tourniquet," he said to Nick. "I got to hold them off."

And he was at one of the windows, firing at the flashes he could see in the timber.

"Pull me over where I can shoot," Nick said, his face white with pain. "God, there must be a army of them out there."

Then, all at once, the firing stopped.

"Maybe got one or two," Slater said, speaking to himself as much as to the boy. "Hard to tell." Then as he was bandaging Nick's wounds he saw that he had been creased along the back of his own hand. Holding the wound to his mouth; he sucked the blood and spat.

"There's a bunch of them down at the corral," he told Nick. And now his eyes cut to Weber.

Weber had managed to roll over on his side. He was staring at Nick and Slater, his face wide open and ashen, his lips hanging apart.

"Cut me loose, Slater. This ain't my fight."

"But you knew it was coming, didn't you!" And he had grabbed Weber by his collar and pulled his head up. "Tell me!"

"I didn't know. I swear it!"

"Tell me straight, damn you!" His hand was now on Weber's windpipe and he started to squeeze.

"Let me loose," Weber gasped.

"Tell me what you were doing out here."

"Slater . . ."

Suddenly he threw him back onto the floor. "Maybe I got to cut it out of you," he said, taking his barlow knife out of his pocket.

"Look—I didn't know they were coming here. I mean, I didn't. I thought they were going to Meeteetse." Weber's eyes were bugging out as he stared at the blade of the barlow.

"Who? You didn't know who was coming here?"

"The army. It's the Association's army. There is fifty of them. Slater, you don't have no chance."

"Why did they come here? Why didn't they just go to Meeteetse?"

"I don't know."

"Yes, you know. That's why you came. Only I reckon you didn't figure on them coming so fast."

"Let me go."

Slater pushed the point of the barlow under Weber's chin. "Tell me the whole story."

The sweat was pouring down Weber's forehead and soaking into his beard. "Farkas," he stammered. "It was Farkas."

"He is with them?"

"He said he would get them to come by here. They had planned to take Meeteetse, wipe out the small cattlemen and anyone sympathizing with them. But Farkas, he wanted to come by here."

"And you were sent to bushwhack me, just to make sure."

Weber tried to speak, but with the knife stabbing under his chin, no more words could come out.

"I ought to kill you," Slater said. "Maybe I will."

"No—not just like that. You wouldn't kill a man like that, Slater."

"Isn't that what you figure a Indian would do, you sonofabitch!"

He turned away and looked out the windows. There was no sign of action from the timber.

Now he sat down by Nick and began checking his weapons and ammunition.

He had his eyes on Weber, reading the man's thoughts. "I am reading it right along with you, Weber. Do not call out or try to make a break. One sound, one move, and I promise I will cut you into pieces."

Now the day broke over the tops of the mountains and the first rays of the sun pierced the leaden sky, washed along the walls and roof of the cabin, and across the meadow and found at last the army waiting in the timber.

Inside the cabin, Slater was trying to make Nick comfortable. Suddenly a voice calling from the trees reached him.

"Slater! We have got you surrounded. Come out with your hands up!"

"You go out there," Nick said, gasping the words, "and you are a dead bird."

"That's what I know."

He stood at one of the windows, waiting, watching. Something sooner or later had to move.

And it did. And his shot was true. The man's cry of pain cut the cool morning air, in testimony to Slater's accuracy, but it was instantly drowned in a crash of rifle fire.

They were shooting from all three sides now. Yet no one dared to try crossing the meadow. They had plenty of ammunition. Enough, as Doc Slocum had observed laconically to Bellows when they had been watching the unloading at Elk Pass, enough to kill everyone in the entire state of Wyoming.

Slowly the sun rode into the sky, a yellow disc behind gray clouds. But no one in the woods knew that. Only the man in the cabin noted it, for he knew that night would come and he wondered if he and Nick would be there to see it.

As the morning wore on, punctuated by a lone shot every so often from the cabin or by massive rifle fire from the trees, the Major grew impatient.

"We have got to get in closer," he said.

"How?" Sweetwater John let fly a stream of saliva onto a bed of pine needles. "Any man tries to get across that clearing'll be dead 'fore a man can scratch his own ass."

"Sooner or later he will have to make a break for it," Frank Domino said.

Hinchy's face was a monument to his anger and frustration. "Sooner or later! How much sooner? How much later? He has killed two men already and wounded three more. Damnit! Goddamnit to hell! We should be in Meeteetse, taking the town!"

"Why not go then?" suggested Slocum, who had been overhearing the discussion. "Leave some men here to hold him, and take the rest to town. There is only Slater and the one who was shot."

"Farkas says that was Nick Dyer," Domino said. "Just a kid."

But the doctor was offering reason to the wrong man.

"Doctor Slocum, I am not abandoning my position because of one man and a boy, or because there are fair-weather soldiers among us!"

"I am not suggesting that, Major . . . Only that it might be prudent to move on to Meeteetse rather than to allow ourselves further delay." He held up his hand in a gesture of self-effacement. "I am not a military man."

"Precisely," the Major said. "And now, sir, if you would attend to the wounded . . ." He turned to Domino and

Sweetwater John. "Gentlemen, we will do our duty. I intend to take that cabin before nightfall. Well before nightfall."

"We will get him," Frank Domino said, and he gave a nod at his own words.

So far they had only gotten him along the back of his hand, and across his left cheek with a piece of flying window glass. But they had sure gotten Nick.

"I am done for," the boy was saying. "You better make a run for it. We don't have a chancet."

"Someone will hear the shooting and will ride to town."

"Piss-poor likely," replied the boy.

He was at one of the windows again. With one swift, flowing movement he raised the rifle and fired.

"Can't tell if I got him," he said.

He stood looking down into the gray face of the boy. "If we can hold them, word is bound to get to town. We hold 'em here, the town will have a chance."

"Slater!" a voice called. "You do not have a chance, Slater. We have got a hundred men out here and we can wait a month." It was Sweetwater John Hillman.

He waited a moment and then slipped to the window. But there was no chance to fire.

"Slater," the voice called again. "You can get Nick to town. He is hurt bad. Come on out. You got no chance at all!" And then, following a pause, "We got a doctor right here, Slater. Come on out, you and the boy!"

Now it was quiet. He stood looking down at the boy. Nick was lying on his back, with his eyes staring up; his breathing was hardly visible. His face was the color of faded denim.

Slater crossed to his bedroll and took out a dog-eared

copybook and a stub of pencil. Now he squatted on his heels near Nick.

> Me and Nick was just up when the attack started. Weber is with us. He is a spy for the Association. Boys, there is fifty men out there.

He licked the end of the pencil and continued slowly.

> Nick is shot but not dead yet. He is awful sick. I must go and wait on him.

17

Old Ridey Durham, much against the protest of his granddaughter, had every intention of working the roundup.

"Man keeps young working," he had put it. "Not by settin' on his fat bee-hind."

And with this in view he had decided to ride out to take another look at his cabin near the North Fork on Spring Creek. The cabin could be used, he had told Slater, as a camp or headquarters for the men when they started the gather. The true fact was, he felt a tiny fear that maybe Slater and the others might figure him too old for working cattle and he was anxious to establish himself as a part of things early. Hell, maybe he couldn't no longer peel a bronc or bust a calf, but he could sure heat a iron.

He had ridden out of town around noon, figuring to spend the night at his cabin or maybe with Slater.

Around mid-afternoon as he was topping the lip of a draw just below the Circle E he heard rifle fire.

"Sounded like a whole damn army," was how he told it

to Clay Joyner and the men at the Pastime after he had reached there on a lathered horse.

"You see them?" the sheriff asked. "See how many?"

"Didn't get too close. But I know only Slater and Nick is out there; but them others, them rifles sounded like it was the cavalry and a Injun surround!"

Clay Joyner looked grave. He had just come into the saloon to call some of the men to a meeting at his office. Alarming news had come over the telegraph wire which had been out for two days. When Ridey burst in he had only finished telling the gathering about the special train that had left Cheyenne the previous afternoon.

"It is them," Joyner said. "No doubt on that. They must've swung by to take Slater 'fore they came here."

"Then we are lucky," Charley Carew said. "We have time to get ready to defend ourselves."

"We better get on out and help Slater and Nick," Ridey Durham insisted.

"Have you telegraphed the militia?" Clarence Cohoes asked the sheriff.

"I have. I am waiting for an answer." Clay Joyner scratched the back of his head, his eyes on Ridey Durham. He did not like at all what he had to say. "Boys, get all available guns and ammunition and anyone can handle same. I am putting on a curfew. Get all the children and women off the street." He turned to the man beside him. "Lon, I want deputies. A lot of 'em. I'll swear 'em over at my office. Harry, I want you to send another message to the Army, right to Colonel Swayles." He looked quickly at Ridey Durham and was going to go on but the door of the saloon opened and a tall man entered.

"What's this I hear about an invasion of Big Horn County, Joyner?" The speaker wore no hat, and across the top of his bald head ran a half-dozen strings of dark, wet hair.

"Mayor, we got the news over the telegraph. 'Pears now the line was down from being cut, not from the storm. Ridey here was up by the North Fork and heard plenty of rifle fire at the Circle E. It has got to be them."

"And they will be here next," said someone.

The mayor stood now in the center of the group. "By when do you reckon they will reach Meeteetse?"

"Depends," Joyner said. "But we cannot wait. We must act quickly." He was speaking to the mayor's back, for the latter had stepped swiftly to the bar.

"Tom, give me a whiskey." Then, turning to Joyner, "You have tried the Army?"

"Hell, Mayor," said Clarence Cohoes. "You know the militia does what the Association tells 'em. They ain't going to help us. The Cheyenne bunch got them right in their britches pocket."

"Then we had better help ourselves. We had better barricade the town." And he signaled the bartender for a refill.

"What about Slater?" Ridey said, raising his voice.

"God help him," said someone standing near the door.

"How about us helping him?" said Ridey, and there was anger in his voice.

More men had entered the saloon now as the news spread.

Clay Joyner said, "Ridey, I don't know how to say this . . . but it is eighteen miles to the Circle E, and there is more than fifty men in that bunch, according to the message we got. I hate to say it, but Slater don't have a chance."

"Goddamnit, get me a posse and I'll ride right through them sidewinders!" The old man was almost stomping with anger.

"Hell," said Clarence Cohoes. "We go riding out to Slater's, we will spread ourselves so thin they will just pick us off. Our best chance is to fort up the town and be ready for them when they come."

"I agree to that," Charley Carew said. And there were murmurs and exclamations of agreement through the gathering.

"It makes sense," the mayor said. "We wouldn't get there till sunup, and by then it will be all over."

"Might be right now," someone said. And this brought a pause to the group.

But Ridey Durham was not finished. "Slater is the head of us cattlemen," he said. "And you are just leaving him and Nick out there to be kilt. You cowards!" And he whipped off his hat and threw it on the floor.

"We got to think of the women and children," Clay Joyner said.

And the mayor added, "Those are professional gunmen out there. Not cow waddies."

The old man stood facing them, his chest heaving, his fists clenched at his sides. Watching him, Clay Joyner almost changed his mind.

"We got to see it clear, Ridey," he said. "Sure, we can ride out and try to help Slater. But what good would that do the rest of the town? You know he is probably done for by now. We would only get ourselves in a helluva tight and lose the town." He shook his head. "I want to go. I know how you feel."

"Then why'n hell don'cha! Slater's out there right now, savin' our ass, goddamnit!"

"Our duty is here," Clay Joyner said softly. His words were not strong in the face of the old man's demand and he felt it. But now as he heard the echo of what he had just said a sort of strength came to him and he spoke in a different voice. "I was elected to keep the peace here. The women and children must come first. For all we know, that Hinchy could be another Quantrill or Bloody Bill Anderson, and maybe some of you recollect how those boys burned Lawrence and a few other towns and what happened to the women."

Ridey Durham spat furiously at the nearest cuspidor, almost streaking the mayor's polished boots as he did so. Now his voice was quieter as he said, "And if the mayor here was out there 'stead of Slater? Or if it was Clarence or Carew?"

His accusation brought a silence to the room. And it stayed there while he put his cap on and walked out.

18

> It is now about six hours since the first shots. Nick is still alive. They are still shooting and are all around the house. Boys, there is bullets coming in here like hail.

He wrote slowly, laboriously, for he was unused to it and the pencil stub was small in his calloused hand. Weber lay on his side, watching him. He had only spoken once more and that was to ask for water, which Slater had given him.

A wind had sprung up in the early afternoon and now the firing was desultory.

Then, as he was moving back from one of the windows, his leg gave way. Luckily the bullet had gone on through, missing his thigh bone. Quickly he tore up a shirt and made a tourniquet.

Nick lay with his eyes closed. He was barely breathing. Slater could just see the one button on his shirt moving.

> It is afternoon. I am hurting. My leg is sore and stiff and I have lost some blood. I got it in the shoulder

too. Still got some ammunition for the Winchester, no more for the Henry. Got three shells for the Colt.

He put down the copybook and the pencil and rolled a smoke. It was quiet. Watching Nick, the button on his shirt, he remembered the time Fox, the dun gelding, had thrown the boy when he was out wrangling one day. He must have been twelve, thirteen, and he had walked the horse home and Slater had eaten into him. He had not wanted to spoil him by letting him buck anymore, Nick had said, so he had walked back leading Fox. But Slater had cussed him for letting the horse think he was afraid.

But then—that spring, was it?—when the crazy white mare had tried to kill the boy when he'd been roaching her mane and he had held on to her even though she'd pulled the crosspiece right out of the hay bin and had drug him plumb out into the corral, rearing up trying to tromp him with her forefeet; and Nick had stuck right with her till she'd quieted some; and then he'd gentled her and led her back into the barn. And himself and Ridey had seen it. Ridey had said how the kid had his guts all right.

He looked now at the button on Nick's shirt. And he picked up the copybook and pencil.

Nick is dead.

While in the timber, Major Hinchy was saying, "I want that cabin fired this afternoon."

"You are asking for some men to be shot," Frank Domino told him. "They will have to push the wagon and that means they will show themselves."

"Then call for volunteers."

"I don't reckon you will get any, Major."

Hinchy snorted. "Not if they have your attitude." He patted his thigh while his forehead wrinkled. "What about that man, what is his name—Farnum, Parker?"

"Farkas."

"Bring him here."

When Farkas had been brought, Hinchy said, "You were so all-fired eager to make this detour that it occurs to me you might want to do something constructive about getting Slater." He waited, watching Farkas's eyes narrow. "In other words, I am prepared to give you another chance."

"Major, I will do anything to get—to bring Slater to justice," Farkas said, returning to some of his former self-assurance. And too, the Major noted, to a certain insolence which he had not revealed while they were still on the train.

"I want that cabin fired this afternoon, Farkas. You will need to get your own volunteers." He looked at Domino. "I do not believe it will be easy."

"I will get them, Major. I know the Texans."

From the window Slater could see some of the preparations. And now he watched as the wagon was pushed away from the trees. It was filled with branches and dry hay and the men were hidden behind it. It was not yet fired, but as it moved, a wave of bullets poured at the cabin.

Someone shouted, "Put a match on it now!"

But he could see legs. He fired and a scream of pain marked his success. He fired again. And again. And the wagon was suddenly abandoned as the men fled for cover.

His hands were shaking as he poured cold coffee into a mug and drank. He sat there in the cabin with his back to the cold stove while overhead the sun, screened by massive clouds, moved toward the end of the day.

"Slater . . ." It was Weber.

He did not answer.

"Slater for God's sake . . . !" Weber could hardly control his voice. "They fire this cabin, you got to cut me loose!"

"Shut up," Slater said.

Building a smoke now, his hands steadied. Ah, that smoke was good. The coffee was good. He wished he had some whiskey, but Nick had finished the bottle.

And again that summer came to him, as it had that night when he had lain in his bedroll out on the pine needles. That summer when he had met her and when she had left at the end of it. And then when she came back and he had watched her eyes sadden; and he heard the stories about Frank Farkas and it had made him hot with anger.

Then that time at the Fourth of July shindig when she had suddenly come up and said hello to him. And Farkas had come up after and accused him of things and called her names right in front of the whole crowd and it had all at once burst in him and he had beaten Frank Farkas real good.

And he had not seen her for a whole year. By then Farkas was gone—with some woman, threatening to kill that damn Injun Slater on sight if he ever ran into him, which he had for near a whole year taken good care not to.

So they had started to see each other and it was like it

had been. Almost. For there was still Farkas even though he was not around, and no one knew where he was; and pretty soon the shadow talk got started, the wicked, wagging tongues. Not only was she a married woman, he more likely than not was a damn Indian. Frank Farkas might be a drunk, a thief, a liar and cheat, even a gunman —but he was at least white.

And with Slater you could not be sure. Sure, he looked white, but he acted like a damn Indian. Hadn't he lived with them, been raised by High Eagle's Shoshones? Hell, he might as well be one of them.

She did not feel that way, of course, but she would not move out to the Circle E. She would not live openly with him as his woman, because of the child. The child was not yet born, but it must not be born into that, she said. Into the gossip and slander. She was not turning from him, she only wanted to wait a little longer. It was the child she was thinking of. The child had to come first.

While outside the cabin the shadows grew long on the meadow as the sun moved closer to the edge of the sky.

Now the clouds opened and a light breeze sprang up, clearing the sky to a sapphire blue. Across the valley, the sun was dazzling on the great snowcapped peaks. A jay called somewhere. And from far off came the bark of a coyote.

Save for an occasional spasmodic, almost casual burst, the firing had stopped. Four of the Invaders lay dead and five others had been wounded. As the day drew to a close, the long rays of the dying sunlight lighted the side of the mountain and seemed to warm the little meadow and the beleaguered cabin.

Slater saw it on the windowsill, followed it as it spilled

across the pine floor and touched Nick, who was lying by the stack of stove wood.

> I heard them splitting wood. I guess they are going to try to fire the house again with another wagon tonight. Maybe they found that stack of pitch-pine posts out by the spring. I think I will make a break when night comes if alive.

He watched the sunlight slip away from Nick and back out of the cabin; and all at once he saw himself as a boy fishing the Greasy Grass in the late afternoon with Little Bear and Owl.

He felt it cold on his hands now, and then as the breeze stirred he smelled the clean, fresh meadow. With a start he realized that there was only half a bucket of water left in the cabin. Not much use for fire fighting. Not that it mattered, even if he had twenty buckets.

> Boys, I feel pretty lonesome now. I wish there was someone friendly with me so we could watch all sides at once.

There was a pot of cold stew on the stove and as he ate he realized how hungry he had been. The pot was about the only thing in the cabin that had not been hit.

When he was finished he crossed to Weber and untied his hands so he could eat. But Weber had no appetite.

"You gonna loose my legs, Slater?"

But Slater did not answer him.

It was night now and the moon rose in a velvet sky. Not very helpful if he tried to slip out. On the other hand, he knew they would be fearful of moving in the meadow so long as he could see.

He could make out the abandoned wagon clearly. It stood at the edge of the timber, piled high with branches and dry hay, waiting for the torch and the men to push it.

Carefully, he sighted the Winchester, standing well to the side of the window so as to offer no target. He pulled the trigger. The bullet slammed into the wooden axle of the wagon. He got off a second shot that also scored, but a barrage drove him back.

He waited, then moved to the other window and fired.

"The sonofabitch has busted the axle," someone shouted. And he could hear the others cursing in the trees.

Suddenly a voice rose from the timber.

"Slater! It's me—Farkas. Frank Farkas. Remember me, you Injun bastard!"

He felt something twist inside him, almost like a sickness.

"Slater!" the voice called. "Come on out, or it won't be just you who will be sorry!" And Farkas screamed out a river of profanity at the cabin. He shouted all of it, all the detailed filth that certain men live with.

"My God!" said Slocum.

Hinchy was furious. "Arrest him!" he ordered Sweetwater John Hillman. "Tie him up. Gag him. And this time he will stay tied!"

Sweetwater John and two of the ranchers stepped toward Farkas, who was still screaming at the man in the cabin. One swift blow from Sweetwater John and Farkas slumped to the ground.

"Let him cool," said Sweetwater John, rubbing the barrel of his Deane & Adams along his thigh and then neatly holstering it.

Hinchy called an immediate council of war. "I want that cabin fired! One man—one man is not going to stop us! And I do mean that!"

"The second wagon is almost ready, Major. We can move in pretty soon now."

Then Slocum said, "Can we not wait until the moon is down, sir? My God, there has been enough killing for one day."

Major Hinchy did not answer.

In the pause that followed they heard Morley swearing. "That damn Farkas stole my last bottle of whiskey, damn him!"

Now, in the cabin, Slater settled down on his bedroll, which he had moved to the stove. He wished he had some whiskey. The moon was on the windowsill and he looked at it, thinking, they will send in another wagon as soon as it is dark.

He felt drowsy now. His leg was hurting badly, and so was his shoulder. If only he could chance some sleep he would feel better. He had better not. He had better stay awake. He had to stay awake. It was not bad sitting there on the bedroll. It would be so nice to just close his eyes.

He looked over at Nick. Well, he will get a hot burial, he thought. And himself too. And Weber. His head was aching. Had he been hit? He felt his head and looked at his fingers. No blood.

For a moment a crazy hope caught at him. Could he get away? Not with that leg and shoulder. But could he maybe hold out till help came from town? They must surely know by now. And he was surprised to find himself asking: Was that what it meant to die well, to go on hoping to live? And he found his thoughts again on his early years. No, it did not mean that. That was not what it meant.

He had watched High Eagle die. It was something never to forget. The chief had been an old man and he had predicted the time of his own death. And when the time came all the leaders of the tribe came together. And he had been sent for. A messenger had come to Laramie, where he was topping out broncs. And he had come.

The chief lay on buffalo robes. He was very close to death. His eyes were closed, but he was breathing. Slater was looking at the scar on the old man's cheek when suddenly his eyes opened. They were as bright as ever they had been, and Slater had felt something dissolve all through him as they met his.

Looking at him, High Eagle spoke. "I see that you are still the Man of Two Places. It is too bad. I ask you to see my death, for when you were little I told you it is important to know how to die well."

He had felt High Eagle's eyes holding him, like a grip, and then they looked at the others standing near him, each one in turn. And then, even while those eyes were still open, something behind them closed, and was finished. And it was forever.

A bullet suddenly slammed through the window and tore the stovepipe from its hook. It fell to the floor with a crash.

It did not matter. He saw now that nothing mattered. He would do what had to be done. There was no escape. And he knew now there would be no rescue. He had always been alone and he would be so to the end. There was nothing he could do about that. Still, it would have been good to settle one or two things. But what could a man do? There wasn't a thing you could do about it. Only a man had to keep going, he saw. He opened his eyes wide. Yes. A man had to keep going. A man who had been born had to die.

And right now a bullet slammed into the shelf of mason jars on the wall above Weber. Glass spilled all over the man, who was cowering in terror.

"Slater . . . my God, please . . . !"

Slater was on his feet. He crossed quickly to the man in the corner and began to cut his bonds. Was there time? There had to be time.

"Get your legs and arms moving," he said. "Then take that hammer and start pulling up those floor boards." He nodded to the rear wall. "Then take that shovel and start to dig."

I had forgot about the half-done root cellar. I will have to cover Weber digging with rifle fire. But I am getting low on ammo.

19

The day came like a whisper. The sun was not yet above the mountaintops, but light was reaching from behind the great rimrocks in back of the cabin, now lighting the great mantle of snow on the high peaks across the valley, at first in soft blue but now turning to glittering gold and white. In the immense sky a lone eagle soared, his great wings spread wide as he gave himself effortlessly to the current that was there.

The tunnel was finished. Weber was totally exhausted. He lay on his back, sucking deep breaths. He had dug most of the night in the tough hardpan.

And miraculously, Hinchy had held to his idea that a full-scale attack was always better at dawn or dusk. They would wipe out the cabin now, and by evening they would strike Meeteetse.

"How we going to get into the root cellar?" Weber asked Slater. "I ain't actually dug that far."

"They fire the cabin there'll be a lot of smoke, a lot of confusion," Slater explained. "It is only a few steps between the cabin and the side of the mountain. And the rock wall will help on the heat," he added.

He crossed from where he had been standing at the window and began tying Weber's legs.

"What the hell are you doing?"

"I got to see what kind of job you done."

"I told you, I got all the way through."

But Slater was tying his hands.

He could hear them close outside now. His leg was stiff and sore, and so was his shoulder, but he got down and worked his body through the hole that Weber had dug. Yes—he could make it. With luck. He drew back into the cabin now.

His shoulder was throbbing, and his leg felt as if it was on fire. The bandages were dark with hard blood, but he did not consider changing them. As he stood by the window he went out of focus. His head swam. But he went to the bucket and threw water on his face.

Only there was no time. He could hear them right outside now.

"Come cut me loose," Weber begged. "Give me a gun to fight with at least."

And time was passing. He could hear their voices now as they grew bolder. Swift as his leg permitted, he stepped toward Weber. He bent to cut Weber's bonds, and as he did so a barrage of rifle shots swept over his head, just missing him. Weber let out a little cry and slumped forward. He had been shot through the head. Slater saw that the bullets had almost torn his head from his shoulders.

Now, almost fumbling in his haste, but telling himself not to hurry, remembering High Eagle's saying never to do anything quickly, but slowly and well, he began taking off his clothes. It was hard dressing Weber, but he got it done just as the wagon crashed into the door of the cabin.

Oh—let there be time! When he got to the window he saw that they were right there. He could smell the burning hay and pitch. Painfully, he raised the Winchester and pulled the trigger. On an empty chamber. Suddenly he vomited.

Now, with nearly numb fingers, he jacked in ammunition as the flames began to lick around the door. A storm of bullets drove him from the window. From the middle of the cabin, he shot through the burning cabin door.

Suddenly, he heard a voice, at the window to his left. "Slater!" Almost before it reached his ears, he had dropped, rolled, and was up on one knee, firing the Winchester. It was Frank Farkas and Slater's bullets caught him in the throat. Total disbelief was etched on his face as he slumped on the windowsill and fell out of the cabin; the victim more of his own hatred in calling Slater, than of the actual bullets.

The cabin was filling rapidly with smoke. His eyes were watering and he had started to cough, and he could feel the heat on his face and hands. He tried shooting through a window at the men who were partially hidden by the blazing wagon. But he was again driven back by firepower from the timber.

> The house is all fired. Goodbye, boys, if I never see you again.

Somehow he managed to move the table to the back of the cabin and over the hole. He could hardly see, the cabin was so thick with smoke, and water was pouring out of his eyes. The smoke too was tearing at his lungs and he was coughing and gasping and almost out of control of himself as he dragged Weber to the table, and lay him across it. Then he pushed the copybook into Weber's pocket.

He fell to his hands and knees and began crawling into the hole.

He did not feel the cool air striking his face and hands as he dragged himself out into the narrow space behind the cabin. The attackers were all at the front of the cabin as he staggered into the root cellar.

20

When Ridey Durham rode up with L. T. Greenough, Swede Pete, and two young boys, the army was gone. They had skirted them down by the river without any trouble. The invaders of Big Horn County had taken their dead with them. They had not tarried over their victory, but had simply left the body they thought was Slater's, and the remains of Nick, and ridden on.

"Where will we bury him?" L.T. asked.

"Right here," said Ridey. "The two of them." The old man knelt down. He paused for a moment and then turned the body over. He almost felt sick then, though he had seen plenty in his time. He was about to stand up when he saw a bulge in one of the shirt pockets.

It was the copybook, soaked in blood, but the writing was clear.

Swede Pete looked at the book when Ridey handed it to him. Swede Pete had no teeth so he spoke very seldom.

But now he said, "He was a strange man, that Slater."

"He was a hell of a man," Ridey Durham said, looking at the blood from the copybook on his hands.

Old Ridey Durham had been an Indian fighter and a lot of things and he was long on good sense. He was a man who always listened to what he heard inside himself. And he heard something now as he stood looking down at that body. It was then he remembered the dynamite and his promise to bring some for Slater's root cellar.

He looked up at the sky and then looked down at the body again. While Swede Pete, L.T., and the two boys stared in surprise, he strode to the stone wall that supported the back of the cabin.

"Come here and help me," he called as he crawled into the root cellar.

It was real hot in there, and Slater was out of it. But he was alive.

"I will be a sonofabitch," Ridey said when they had carried him out to the meadow.

Swede Pete spat through his ancient gums. He shook his head ruefully. "He may be part Indian, for sure," he said. "But he is for sure part coyote, and that's a gut."

21

Meanwhile, the Invaders rode, not very quickly, for though they saw themselves victorious, their mood was chastened.

"Not so tasty on the palate," was how Slocum put it. "One man holding off fifty gunfighters for twenty-four hours."

"He ain't holding off anyone right now," one of the Texans observed. But his words were without life.

Matthew Bellows sighed. He was still in severe pain, but he was manfully trying to write up his story of the fight at the Circle E. Morley, on the other hand, was trying to see how he could get to the nearest telegraph office without attracting notice.

As they crossed Slater's bridge over the roaring Greybull, Hinchy spoke. "Mister Domino, we should reach Meeteetse not long after noon at this rate, unless our scouts report something unexpected."

But as they arrived on the other side of the river it was not the scouts who came riding to meet them. It was

Clyde Canton, "Holy" Holley, and Hard Winter Hayes who drew rein on steaming horses.

"The town is all forted up," Canton told the Major, and his eyes were red, especially the one with the cast in it, from lack of sleep. "Joyner has a barricade on each end. They are just waiting for you. What in hell took you so damn long!"

"Hell and damnation!" barked the Major. "We are surely not going to surprise them." And he related briefly to the three men what had happened at the Circle E.

For the first time in some days a smile broke on Clyde Canton's face. "Good work," he said, and he reached to his shirt pocket for his makings.

"Holy" Holley offered a different view. "Appears to me like Slater done some pretty good work," he said sourly, eyeing the wagons with the dead and wounded.

Hard Winter Hayes belched suddenly and scratched the back of his neck. "Anyhow, the man is dead and long overdue, I'd allow. Let us get on with this business."

"We must regroup," Hinchy said. "Is there some place where we can look to the wounded and check our equipment?"

"My outfit's about a hour ride," Hard Winter Hayes said. "But we don't want to spend too much time dallying. You never know but what Swayles and the army might decide to interfere."

"But they are on our side," Canton reminded him.

"That's what I mean. They can come in and take over."

"And let the damn rustlers off," put in Frank Domino. "Send them to the pen or some damn fool thing like that."

"Right." Hard Winter Hayes shifted in his saddle which creaked greatly under his weight.

"What is your plan, Major?" "Holy" Holley asked.

"We will follow my original plan and attack at nightfall. They will be tired after waiting all day. Some will be hungry and want food and drink. They will not be so keen." He paused, drawing his forefinger and thumb along the line of his mustache. "We will split our forces and hit both ends of the town. But you had better give more detail of the town when we make camp." He patted his thigh and allowed his glance to move across the waiting men.

They were relaxed now, at last, chatting and working up their stories of how they had seen the fight at the Circle E. Of course, these accounts would be embellished as time wore on. But for the moment the comments were on the bleak side. Slater had made a hard impression on them.

"We are no heroes, alas," was how Doc Slocum put it. And he began to figure how he could leave the Expedition without causing undue notice.

Now Major Hinchy stood in his stirrups. "Mister Domino, tell the men we will ride to the Double T ranch and make camp. I will call an inspection then, including a complete count of weapons and ammunition."

"Good enough, Major."

Everyone felt better as they mounted up again and rode away from the bridge and the Circle E. The river was behind them, though they would have to cross it again further down, but Slater was finished and so, they figured, was the backbone of rustler resistence.

The town, meanwhile, waited. Clay Joyner had been everywhere—checking weapons, ammunition, assigning men to strategic positions, seeing to the erection of the barricades. He had sent another message to the Army and the mayor had telegraphed the governor.

Now, in the early forenoon as he returned to his office, he was reflecting that by now it was all over for Slater and Nick. And he wondered what had happened to Ridey Durham and the four who had ridden out with him.

He was tired. He had not been in bed or even home in hours and he wondered how his wife was taking the situation. He must go by and see. Now as he opened the door of his office he was thinking how it would be to have some coffee and maybe even forty winks. But he discovered that he had company.

"I have been waiting to talk to you, Mister Joyner," said Molly Durham, getting to her feet.

Clay Joyner held up his hand as though to stop what he knew was coming. "I know what you are going to say, Molly. I told your grandfather the same thing I will tell you . . ."

But she interrupted him. "No—I am not going to ask you to take a posse and ride out to the Circle E."

He saw that it was not, as he had instantly feared, an hysterical woman come to carp at him, but a clear, collected young person who was beyond anything like tears.

"What then?" he asked gently, and he took off his hat.

"I want you to get the soldiers."

"I have telegraphed twice to the Army post and the mayor has telegraphed the governor."

"But when?"

The sheriff looked at the clock on the wall of his office. "Long enough ago to get some answer."

"And you have heard nothing?"

He nodded, looking down.

"I can send another message," he said. "And I will."

"Or a rider."

"Molly, you know the Army isn't going to help us. They believe we are all a bunch of rustlers."

She stood very straight there in the tiny room. "I wonder if they do know the situation, as it really is," she said. "I mean, I wonder if Colonel Swayles understands what is happening here to all of us. After all, it is the Army's job to keep the peace, at least that is how I understand it."

"But don't you see, they are with the Stockgrowers. They feel the small stockmen like Slater and your grandfather, and myself too, and you—are rustlers, outlaws. Don't you see that?"

"I see what my grandfather said you told the men in the Pastime, your reason for not getting up a posse—that this could be another Lawrence, another Quantrill raid. I am a woman and I have a child. And I am not going to sit and wait for some band of murdering hoodlums to burn my home and . . . and all the rest of it!" And she strode to the door.

She was outside on the street before he realized it. He stopped her on the wooden walk.

"Where are you going? What are you up to? This is no time to be foolish, Molly. Believe me."

Her clear blue eyes met his evenly. And she spoke directly to him. "I am riding to the fort to see the colonel."

"No!"

"Don't try to stop me. It is clear that messages aren't going to accomplish a thing. But maybe I can at least shame our so-called protectors into doing their duty." And then she added, and there were tears standing in her eyes, "What Grandpa tried when he spoke to you men in the Pastime—when you just let Slater and Nick do it all for you!" And she turned and ran down the street.

Clay Joyner knew what he had to do then.

When he walked into the Pastime the first man he saw was his deputy Lon Brennan. He was talking to Clarence Cohoes and Charley Carew.

"Lon, Molly Durham is riding to the Army post. You get your ass onto leather and follow her." He turned to Cohoes and Carew. "The town is as ready as it is going to get. I am putting Bramwell in charge and I want six men to ride out with me." He let his eyes play swiftly over the room which had fallen into silence.

Clarence Cohoes put down his glass of whiskey. "I will ride with you."

"And I," said Charley Carew.

And others joined in.

"I only want six men," Joyner said. "If they are on their way here we will surprise them; cut their trail from behind."

"And what if they are still at the Circle E?" someone asked.

Clay Joyner ran his hand along the side of his jaw.

"Well then, by God, we will make them permanent residents of Big Horn County."

As he walked in long strides to the livery stable Clay Joyner still was not sure if it was the best decision, but he knew that it was the only one.

22

This day the sky was gentle. There were no clouds and it seemed now to be spring at last. The snow was melting fast on the breathing ground and in the trees the birds sang their songs.

Slater had let Ridey Durham change his bandages and one of the boys brought water from the spring.

"Wisht I had some whiskey with me," Ridey said. "But when we get to town we will take care of that. I mean the two of us."

They covered the two bodies and placed them, separately, at the edge of the meadow where the sun would not strike them.

"We will bury them later," Slater said. "There is not time now."

Ridey said, "Me and Pete and L.T., we will cut back to town. You can come on slower with the boys. With that leg and shoulder is what I mean."

The two boys were standing, silent in their excitement, ready to do anything they were told. They were young boys, twelve and thirteen about, and none of the men were certain who they were.

Slater had been lying on his back, smoking. Now he sat up, and the pain shot through him, but nobody knew that, no one saw it.

"You still got that dynamite over at Spring Creek?" he asked.

Ridey shifted his tobacco chew swiftly, trying to be ready for what was coming. "Far as I know. Never did get it to you."

"Tell them boys how to get it and bring it to Horsehead Crossing."

Ridey's eyes popped. "Now listen . . ."

"We are wasting time, old man. You know better than that."

Old Ridey spat a bountiful amount of brown juice onto a lingering patch of snow. Then he turned and gave swift instructions to the boys. The towheaded one nodded vigorously and the one with red hair, who had been standing with his mouth open, suddenly closed it.

Curiously, the Invaders had left the two horses in the barn, though they had spooked some and broken loose and were now standing out in the corral.

"There's two shovels," Slater said. "We will cut over by the big butte on Little Fork and if luck helps us we will beat them a good piece to the crossing."

"But you can't ride with that leg," said L. T. Greenough. "I am saying that maybe me and Ridey go on ahead, if you tell us what to do when the boys come. Then you and Pete can come more easy like." He was a stringy man, tall, and not generally given to a lot of talk. He looked at Swede Pete now for support in his suggestion, but Pete was just looking at the ground, sucking his gums.

"You can help me into the saddle," Slater said. He began to get up. "Throw a saddle on the roan. And if you got anything for my Winchester I'd appreciate it."

It was Ridey who obliged.

The cabin had not burned completely. In fact, most of it was still standing. But smoke was still curling up from some of the logs and the floor as they rode away from the ranch.

Like some old men and some small children, Ridey Durham liked to tell what was happening, even though it was already known to everyone else. And so now, as they picked down the steep mountain trail, he was saying, "Thing is, they will not be expecting an attack. And with the dynamite we can sure surprise them."

"But the town is ready for them," L.T. observed. "Why push it? Why not get them there?" And he looked at Slater.

They were on a flat place now, breathing the horses for a minute or two.

"They will also be ready for the town," Slater said. "It could go into one of them long things with a lot of women and children getting hurt."

"This way we kin get it done with fast," said Ridey, kneeing his horse to follow Slater down the trail, chewing vigorously and spitting every now and again.

They rode the rest of the way in silence, reaching Horsehead Crossing at noon.

This was where the Greybull ran shallow between its banks and so it was a good place for stock to cross. It was also the way to Meeteetse. Here, too, the banks of the river were lined with cottonwoods and willows and box elders, affording good cover.

"Not a sign of them," Ridey said.

"They will more than likely stop for a break," said Slater. "And they will be moving slow so as not to get to town before nightfall. And they will be slow too after the fighting they already done." As he felt he was; as he could feel the slowness all through himself. And at the same time, it felt good, it felt clean. Whole.

Ridey bit off a fresh chew of tobacco. "Always did appreciate your way of figuring," he said to Slater.

"I reckon I'd still be in that root cellar if you didn't," Slater said wryly.

This brought a short laugh from the others.

Now they lapsed into another silence which was punctuated by Ridey's random shots of tobacco juice and Swede Pete's vigorous sucking of his gums, which always accelerated whenever he was under pressure. As now.

They had been at the crossing maybe an hour when the boys rode up with the dynamite.

"We skirted them down by Hayes' outfit," the redheaded boy said.

And when neither Slater nor anyone else said anything to this, the towheaded one asked what they could do now to help.

"Dig," Slater said. "The trench must be from there to there." He pointed. Then he told them how wide and how deep to make it.

He could not dig himself and so he found a good spot for cover and lay down to study it out more. He was not sure how many he had accounted for up in the meadow, but he figured at least six must be out of it. That would leave maybe forty-five to deal with. And they were not long on ammunition, himself and the five. It had crossed his mind to send one of the boys to town for help, but he did not. Ridey had said nothing about his efforts in the Pastime to get up a posse, but the presence of the three men and two boys said it loud enough. He would only be losing a good hand if he sent one of the boys into Meeteetse.

And he found himself thinking again of High Eagle and how he had always told him never to rely on anyone else, only on himself.

"You can rely on the tribe," the old chief had said, "except you are not really one of the tribe. You are of two places. And so you must learn to do everything yourself. You have only yourself. But, then, to have your self is to have everything."

He could feel that now, that sense of himself, as he lay waiting at Horsehead Crossing. Would he "die well," like High Eagle? But first he had to live well. For, as he had been taught, life is the preparation for dying. It was therefore important to live well so that you could die well. Yes, he realized, in this I am Indian. And he remembered High Eagle telling him that being Indian was not a matter of blood, but a way of life. It did not matter then where he lived—only how.

At the Double T the men were restless. The Major had held inspection and weapons and ammunition had been checked. The horses had been fed and watered. The wounded had been attended to.

"Mister Hillman, tell the men to prepare to move out."

It was at this point that Doctor Slocum felt he could leave the Expedition with the least furor.

"Major, I strongly suggest that the dead and wounded remain here at the Double T, providing Mister Hayes will agree." And Slocum looked earnestly at Hard Winter Hayes.

They were standing in front of the big ranch house, and some of the Double T hands were cutting out horses in the corral.

"Makes sense," Hayes said. "They will only slow us down."

"And they sure don't help the men's feelings none," observed "Holy" Holley. "Damn! Six dead and ten wounded. I can't believe it!"

"You think you could have done better, sir!" Hinchy was rigid with anger at the slur.

"I sure could not have done worse," said "Holy" Holley, real sour. And yet, he recollected fully that grim moment when right before his own bugging eyes Slater had shot off Tod Collum's thumb.

"Boys—gentlemen," said Clyde Canton, coming in burly and smooth. "Let us not quarrel. I believe too that the dead and wounded will hinder us. They should stay here."

"Agreed," the Major replied. "Mister Domino, appoint an orderly to stay with them." And he added, "Only one man will be necessary. Those who are not too badly hurt can help the others."

Doc Slocum's hopes evaporated. But he rallied. "I feel I should stay behind to treat them, Major. A couple of the men are in serious condition."

"We will need you with us, Doctor," Hinchy replied sternly. "That is, if you've still stomach for the campaign." And without waiting for any reply, he turned away.

But Morley, too, was looking for an opportunity to take off. He was avid to reach a telegraph office where he could wire his story to Chicago.

Now, watching the doctor, understanding what was going on inside him, he had an idea. And when the Invaders rode out of the Double T, Morley remained behind, with Doctor Slocum in attendance. The correspondent had developed "a severe case of piles" and had begged for Slocum to treat him; putting in the added inducement of a favorable story in the *Herald*.

"We have no time to waste while you search for your bag of medicines, Doctor," was how the disgusted Hinchy had put it. "Treat this man, and then you will have to ride fast to catch up with us." He paused, suspicion not yet paramount in his mind, though it was close. "Bellows and Morley can come along in one of the wagons. But you will ride ahead. Remember, sir, you are our only medical man." And he strode to his waiting mount, waving a goodbye with his hat to Canton, "Holy" Holley, and Hard Winter Hayes, who were preparing to ride over to Canton's Z Bar spread to get plans moving on the roundup. Nor were those three eager to have Meeteetse's citizens see them aligned with Hinchy.

Morley, watching them leave, permitted himself a smile at his simple ruse. And Slocum began setting up hospital care for his patients. The dead men had been put in an old ice house; the wounded would be decently cared for. The only question now was how to get a horse and which direction to take so that he could get well away from Hinchy and the Expedition. The doctor foresaw only disaster for the men with whom he had been soldiering. By now he had decided that he would head East.

As the Invaders drew away from the Double T, someone mentioned Morley and his piles and the Major muttered something about "damned dude tenderfoot, by God!"

"But it ain't his feet that is tender," Sweetwater John Hillman whispered to Frank Domino, who smiled.

23

They had finished the trench, and now Slater told them to dig two more. These were to be some distance from each other. He reasoned that it would be better to have three shocks, even though the dynamite would not be greatly concentrated, than one big blow-up, which could misfire.

"They will not know what to expect," Ridey said, reading it out to the others. "Might be a dozen of them trenches for all they will know."

They had just finished the last trench and had set the dynamite when L.T. rode back from his lookout on the other side of the river.

"They are down by the butte," he said. "I'd judge forty, give or take."

"Good enough," Slater said. "Give me a hand up on the roan." And when he was in the saddle, his face white where usually it was dark, and his eyes piercing with pain, he said, "And the Winchester."

"What you doing?" asked L.T.

"I will draw them. I want to make sure they come this

way, not lower down. You will be there—and there, and there." He pointed. "Keep falling back. After L.T. lights the first fuse we got to make sure they don't come on too soon. But not too late either."

He paused, and now quite slowly and deliberately he built himself a smoke. He licked the paper, drawing the cigarette across his tongue a second time after it was rolled. Then he struck a match on his saddle horn.

"They will be excited and confused some after crossing the river, so they won't be watching too close for anything like these here trenches. We will let the point men get by us so that we can get to the main body from the sides. We might work it so they think they're in a surround."

It was what High Eagle had once told him of Crazy Horse when the Sioux chief and his warriors had lured a work detail of whites at Fort Kearny into a trap and wiped them out. Except that he had no warriors behind him, he reflected as he rode out. He had two old men, two boys, and himself. He rode quickly across the river.

Now he saw the first rider. And behind him another. The point riders for sure. He held his rifle ready so that he could shoot from the hip, not wishing to raise it because he wanted to be able to maneuver.

Now they saw him. He kept the Winchester low, out of their line of vision. They had not yet realized who he was. He was still in Weber's clothing. Probably they had him figured as some cowboy rounding up stock or checking feed. He kept his head down until they were close, and then suddenly he looked up, staring squarely at them.

They drew up so short they almost pulled the bits out of their horses' mouths. Slater just looked at them. For them to see the man whom they had supposedly left for dead in the meadow only a few hours before was almost enough to unseat them.

Now he lifted the rifle.

"Drop your guns. And tell them back there that they are surrounded. They better come on with their hands up."

The two men were frozen until he said, "Git!" Then they dropped their weapons on the ground, turned their horses, and cut back down the trail.

He turned the roan now and called to one of the boys to pick up the guns, then he signaled L.T. to light the first fuse.

It was only minutes before he heard them coming. Now he took off his hat and waved it, riding back and forth so that they had a clear view of him. Bullets sang around him now and he pulled back quickly across the river.

And here they were, pounding straight into Horsehead Crossing. He waited again. How close was the flame? Would it go out? Would it catch too soon?

The first horses splashed into the river and the main body of men drove over the crossing, firing as they came. But Slater and the others waited, holding their fire.

The horses had almost reached the first trench when Slater fired. The others followed his signal. He could hear someone shouting orders as they swept by his place of concealment in a thick stand of cottonwoods. They were just past him when the air was torn with explosion. It was too soon to have any serious effect, but it did cause surprise and confusion. Horses reared. Men cursed and fired aimlessly.

Someone was bellowing orders and the attack drove on, as the defenders fell back, firing. The second dynamite hit full center. Horses and men were thrown in the air. They were milling around now as the third line of dynamite exploded harmlessly, though it still had the effect of bringing confusion and even terror to the attackers, who were in such a state that they did not know where to shoot or how to proceed.

Hinchy had been knocked out of his saddle, but he was on his feet, still shouting orders. Sweetwater John Hillman had been shot right through the head, and Frank Domino's gun arm hung helplessly at his side.

It was just at this moment that Clay Joyner and his posse of six rode up. The fight was over. The Invaders, what was left of them—and they still outnumbered Slater and the posse three to one—threw down their guns.

The sun was halfway down the afternoon sky when Major Miles Hinchy, mounted again, rode forward. His shirt was torn, he had lost his hat. And the look on his face when he saw Slater and Clay Joyner with eight men and two boys was something no one ever would forget.

"I will surrender," the Major said, drawing himself up in his saddle, rigid with rectitude, "but not to this man!"

Clay Joyner kneed his horse forward. "I am sheriff of Big Horn County," he said, "and you will damn well surrender to me, mister!"

There was a sudden movement at the rear of the now-bunched Invaders, and Doc Slocum rode forward. He had been creased by a bullet along the jaw and a slow trickle of blood marked the fact.

"I will surrender to this man," he said. "I will surrender to Slater."

24

How long he slept he did not know. He only knew it must have been a long time, for when he awakened in the clean bed in the room with the bright sunlight pouring in he realized that his whole world was different.

Someone handed him a drink of water. It was Doc Slocum.

"Digging lead out of you is like mining," the doctor said. "I bet I found some old pieces you didn't even know were there." He blew his nose suddenly, and went on, wiping, speaking half into an enormous red handkerchief. "But you will live. You will have to stay down a few days. You have lost a lot of blood."

Slater stared at him, trying to place the face.

"I am Elijah Slocum, formerly medical officer in Major Miles Hinchy's—uh—ill-fated Expedition into Big Horn County. I have offered my services, which were accepted by Meeteetse's resident physician, Doctor Raines, since he was clearly shorthanded."

"How long have I been here?"

"Two days. You came on Thursday. It is now Saturday."

"Damn—we will miss the gather."

Ridey Durham now stepped into his line of vision. "What he needs, Doc, is a little touch of whiskey. Whiskey is known to replace blood even before it gets lost."

Slocum winced. "If you want to kill him, and I am not sure that is at all possible, then go ahead. I am only a doctor, and," he added, "a prisoner."

Ridey grunted at that.

Slater said, "Tell me where we are at."

Slocum, usually garrulous, deferred to the old man, and Ridey told how, as they were riding into town, word came that Colonel Swayles was on the way with the Army and that the town was under martial law.

"Molly done it," he said admiringly. "That girl could talk a rattler out of striking, by God." He offered the bottle now which he had taken from an enormous pocket in his trousers.

The liquor reached every part of his body, like a hot wind. He lay back and just let everything go.

"Be careful," Slocum said, himself accepting the bottle. And downing a handsome portion.

And then the doctor said suddenly, as though the liquor had loosened him, which it probably had, "Someone rode back to the Double T with the news that you were still alive. Funny. It was that, I guess, which changed my mind about pulling out for back East, and I rode hell-for-leather to do whatever it was I was supposed to do." He let his eyes run over Slater's prone body. "This, I reckon."

"What about Canton and them?" Slater asked. His head ached, and he was keeping his eyes closed.

"Canton, Holley, and Hayes, and the Association will

stand trial," Ridey Durham said. "'less they can purchase their way out."

"Which is more than not unlikely," Slocum added.

"But we busted them, by God!" Ridey said, suddenly loud. "And by God, we will drink to that!" And he took a vigorous draft from the bottle.

Slocum said, "The story is on the wires. The whole country will have it soon, maybe has it already. Young Morley got it out. He almost missed on you not being dead though." Slocum was thinking about poor Matthew Bellows, who had been thoroughly scooped. But that was life, after all, as he saw it; if you were not a winner, then you were a loser. And he accepted the bottle from Ridey, Slater having refused the round.

He lay there, drowsy, feeling himself for pain. Finding none, he sat up. His head spun, but he remained, and it cleared.

"You had better stay lying down," Slocum said, turning to the door, his eyes and his whole face were glowing with the pleasure of the liquor. "I must go and attend to my other patients."

When he had left the room, Slater said, "Where are my clothes?"

"You are supposed to stay in bed," Ridey told him.

"Get my clothes."

The old man knew better than to argue. He helped Slater get dressed and even helped him take a step or two.

"I have got it now."

"You start that bleeding going fast again and you are in trouble."

"Trouble?"

And the old man coughed out a laugh at that. "Where are you off to?" he asked Slater. "S'pose you think you will make it out to your outfit or something smart like that."

"I am off to get your granddaughter and take her out to my ranch," Slater said, ignoring the old man's sense of humor. "You could go ahead on up to your house and tell her to get herself ready, if you've a mind to."

Ridey Durham gave him a funny look then. "You sure don't know everything, do you, son, even if you are as hammerheaded as I ever seen in my whole lifetime, by God."

He had stopped at the door of the room and turned carefully to face the old man. He was trying to not make any fast moves.

"Meaning?"

"Meaning someone so all-fired smart as you ought to've figured whose house this is by now. I mean, you been awake a whole damn hour!"

And the old man did not spoil his play by smiling.

And then he heard a door open and close below and steps coming up the stairs. He stood looking at Ridey. In a moment the door of the bedroom opened quietly.

Slater said, "I want you to come out to the Circle E, soon as I get everything built up."

She let her hand fall slowly from the doorknob as she stood looking at him. Her eyes went to her grandfather, and then returned to Slater.

"Why do we have to wait till then? I told Grandpa this morning I was planning on leaving when you were ready."

Slater said, "I am ready."

And as he walked along the street with her beside him he felt the sun warm on his back and shoulders, and inside him too. And at last he knew he was no longer a man of two places. But of one.

25

Well, I am pretty sure that is about the straight of it. That is how it all came out. Hinchy and the Invaders were subpoenaed, but they never did come to trial; they just sort of faded out of the country. You know how it is where there is money in the right places.

But the small stockmen won. They got their brands registered and they started building their herds. And sometimes all these years later, maybe when the winter wind is driving down from the Big Horns or when the spring calves are bawling and maybe there's a moment to set and turn things over a bit, out there in the beautiful land, or down in town with a drink or two, at the Pastime or Silver Dollar, someone sure enough will mention Slater and what he did. And sometimes people even go to the town hall in Meeteetse and look at the old copybook, all dark from his blood, but a lot of it still clear enough to read.

I guess no one really ever knew Slater, least not any white man. Maybe Molly Durham did, I don't know. I know some Indian, could have been High Eagle, put it that being Indian was not where you were born but how you lived. I believe it was like that with Slater. He had himself and that was all he needed, is how I see it.

And like old Ridey Durham said, he was a hell of a man. And I say that. A man. He sure will not be forgotten. Not in Wyoming. And for sure not by his son.